Promises HURT

ELLE BROOKS

Printed in the United States of America
First Edition: July 2014
Library of Congress Cataloging-in-Publication Data
  Brooks, Elle
   Promises Hurt / Elle Brooks – 1st ed
    ISBN-13: 978-0-9929888-1-4

   1.   Promises Hurt—Fiction 2. Fiction—Romance
       3.   Fiction—Contemporary Romance

https://www.facebook.com/**elle.brooks.author**

I wasn't planning on falling for Ethan Jamison, hell I wasn't planning on our paths ever crossing. He's the most popular guy at school and a complete player. Me; I'm the perpetual good girl, trying to carry out one last request. But when you make a promise, how far do you go to see it through?

It's a running joke that I'm a terrible liar, if only people knew the truth. My whole life has been spent making excuses and deflecting questions. I was pretty good at it until Blair Thomas entered my world. She saw through the mask that everyone is so willing to accept. She makes me want to tell her all my secrets, but can she promise to keep them?

Ethan

Set a goal SO BIG that you can't achieve it until you grow into the person who can.

-Unknown

Prologue

Blair

2011, age 15

I'M SITTING IN the medical center waiting room swinging my legs back and forth while my best friend, Em, has a blood sample taken. We're supposed to be going to some pizza place that Em wants to try out after this. She overheard Ethan Jamison talking about how he likes to eat there, so now, of course, we have to go there too. Her obsession with him is beyond me; he walks around school like he owns the place. Sure, he's good looking, but if you ask me arrogance is not an attractive feature; neither is hooking up with a new girl every week.

The waiting room smells like bleach and I've already flicked through the pile of out-of-date magazines on the sideboard. You'd think that someone would change them at least a few times a year, but apparently not. These places are depressing; the faded yellow walls and drab green curtains look like they've seen better days. Considering that it's a waiting room and people have to sit here for what feels like forever, the designer could have put in comfy seating, but the ancient-looking plastic seats are only marginally better than sitting on the floor.

Emily had complained to her mom that she was feeling tired all the time, so here we are, trying to figure out if she has an iron deficiency or something. I think if she'd told her mom that we stay up online every night past midnight talking, she wouldn't have been so hasty to bring her to the doctor. I'm pretty sure it's a Facebook addiction she's suffering from and not a lack of iron.

"Hey, that took forever," I say as Em and her mom, Pam, round the corner. Em's face is set in a scowl as she holds a cotton bud to her arm. She's pretty even when she's in a foul mood, which by the looks of it, she is now. I've always wanted to look like her, with that sun-kissed skin and silky blonde hair.

"Oh my god, Blair, that nurse was brutal. I'm pretty sure she pushed that needle in way too far. I thought it was gonna pop out the other side," Emily huffs as she takes a seat beside me.

"Emily, don't be so dramatic!" Pam scolds as she walks over to the sideboard and collects a pile of magazines before sitting down.

I smile and nudge Em's good arm, nodding my head in her mom's direction. She's leafing through a copy of Men's Health.

"I'm sure she's only looking at the articles," I say, wiggling my eyebrows as Emily's draw down in disgust.

"Mom, will you please stop perving in public?" she practically shouts across the room. I bust out laughing as Pam's face reddens and the handful of patients sitting in the waiting area turn in their seats to look.

"Honestly you two, you're terrible!" she says, shaking her head and placing the magazine beside her, replacing it with Good Housekeeping.

It's forty-five minutes before Emily's name is called to go see the doctor again. She stands and motions for me to follow, as Pam throws her plastic water cooler cup into the trashcan.

"Come on in with us, it's horrid sitting in here," she says, as Pam nods her head in agreement.

We are led into Dr. King's office as two other male doctors walk in behind us and take their seats. I have a sudden feeling that this doesn't seem normal—why are there other doctors in here? The atmosphere in the room is almost tangibly thick. The room feels stark and cold; there are no pictures except for a few framed certificates. The walls are pale gray and the sun is casting shadows through the gaps in the ugly blue blinds. I think I actually preferred the waiting area. Pam's shoulders stiffen as she takes in the surroundings, particularly the two men who are sitting to the side. Dr. King makes her way around the desk and looks back and forth between Emily and me before continuing.

"Mrs. Wilson, Emily; perhaps I could speak with you in private?" she asks, giving Pam a look I can't quite read.

"No, Mom, Blair can stay. I want her here," Em says, lacing her fingers through mine and squeezing my hand ever so slightly. I can feel a small tremble and I'm officially panicking at Dr. King's suggestion that I leave.

"Blair is practically family, she can be present if that's okay with you," Pam answers quietly as we all take our seats.

"Very well," she says as she moves papers around her cluttered desk. I'm sure she's stalling and it only ramps my nerves up further. Emily feels it too; her hand is starting to feel clammy against mine.

"We have examined Emily's blood results," she begins, and I can see from the corner of my eye that Pam's holding her breath. "Emily's white blood cell count is not what we would expect it to be for a fit and healthy fifteen-year-old girl. Her neutrophils, which potentially indicate how her immune system is functioning, are extremely low. We would expect to see them at around seven, and currently Emily's are at point zero six." She pauses for a second as she removes the stethoscope she has draped around her neck and places it carefully on the desk in front of her.

"Okay...what does that mean?" Pam asks in a shaky voice as she moves her arm and rests her hand on Em's knee. Emily is steadily increasing the pressure of her grip on my hand and I'm squeezing back just as hard. There is a strange undercurrent running through the room, and I'm sure something bad is about to happen.

"Mrs. Wilson, Emily...from what we can see from the blood results, we are concluding," she gestures to the other doctors in the room, "that Emily has Acute Lympho-blastic Leukemia."

The exhale Pam lets out echoes throughout the death-ly silent room. I'm sitting frozen in fear at the words I've just heard spoken. My face starts to heat up and my eyes prickle as I feel the tears begin.

"Leukemia, as in cancer, Mom? Is that what they're saying? They think I have cancer?" The words come out in a rush and are immediately followed by a terrified sob as Em's body folds in on itself. She still hasn't let go of my hand as her mom falls to her knees from her chair and draws her into a hug, shushing her. I look back to Dr. King whose face looks devoid of any emotion. How can she look like that? I don't understand—how can she deliver the worst possible news anyone can be told and not break down?

"Mrs. Wilson, you'll have lots of questions that I'm sure you will want answered but I'm going to give you these pamphlets that explain everything you need to know about the disease. I'm sure whatever I tell you at the moment will be forgotten in the midst of high-running emotions. I'm going to call for an ambulance to transport you to the Teenage Oncology Unit at UCLA Health Center. I think it's vital that we order more tests on Emily right away to confirm the diagnosis."

Emily hasn't looked up from her mom's shoulder and her sobs feel like a sledgehammer to my heart, each one shattering it into more and more pieces.

"Confirm the diagnosis…so, are you saying you might be incorrect, it might not be cancer? You only did one blood draw, it could be wrong, couldn't it?" Pam's voice is laced with desperation, her eyes wide and glazed over with tears.

"I can't say at this stage that it is categorically leukemia, but I can tell you that we are fairly positive that this is what we are dealing with." She leans forward and passes a handful of tissues over the desk. "We are going to step outside for a moment and give you a few minutes to let the news settle, then we can discuss the next steps." They rise in unison and one by one the doctors leave the room. I find myself wanting to scream, punch, and tear this whole horrid room apart. This isn't right. She can't have cancer—

we're only fifteen.

Emily's sobs stop as she draws back from her mom and looks at her. Tears have stained her cheeks and mascara has smudged a dirty grey line under her red-rimmed eyes.

"Momma, am I going to die?" She sounds completely broken. I'm not sure if it's because she actually is, or because I can hear the blood rushing in my ears. I suddenly feel overwhelmingly dizzy. I imagine this is what an out-of-body experience is like. I don't feel like myself, I feel as though I'm watching this unfold from somewhere else. The sound of heartbreak is clear in Pam's voice as she tries to comfort Emily, but I can't help noticing that she didn't say no.

My body shudders as a chill races down my spine; every nerve ending feels like it's on fire. Surely this can't be happening.

"Don't think like that, Em, You'll be fine," I tell her, although there's not much conviction in my voice. "Whatever happens, it will all work out okay, you'll see."

She looks at me with the most petrified expression I've ever seen, I'm sure it will haunt me for the rest of my life. "You promise?"

I stiffen at her question; I'm not in the habit of making promises that I can't keep. I cross my fingers and silently pray to myself that my next words will turn out to be the truth. "Yes Em." I tell her. "I promise."

Chapter 1

Blair

Present

I SEE A car pull into the drive from my spot on the sofa. It's a quarter after one and I'm finishing up my calculus homework before I head over to see Emily. My stomach drops as I see the person getting out of the mystery car—Em's nurse.

I close my laptop and make my way to the front door to greet her, feeling as though I'm on autopilot. My whole body is full of dread as I open the door and make eye contact with a very somber-looking Carla.

"I'm afraid I have some sad news, Blair. Maybe we should go inside so you can sit down."

I realize I'm just standing in the doorway unable to move; I haven't even said hello. I'm not sure that I trust my voice not to break if I speak. There's only one reason she would be here.

My hands immediately start to feel sweaty and a knot

forms in my throat, restricting the amount of air I can take in and it feels as if my lungs are about to combust.

"She's died, hasn't she?"

All I can focus on is that I wasn't there for her. I was supposed to go see her last night but I had so much schoolwork I put it off until this afternoon. Nurse Carla takes my clammy hand in hers and squeezes ever so slightly, her expression grim and full of sorrow.

"Yes, sweetie, she died yesterday at home where she wanted to be, with her family. I'm so, so sorry, Blair."

The sob that I've been trying like hell to hold onto is ripped out of me and I gasp for a breath while Carla leads me back into the living room. I feel like I'm about to crumble as I make my way across the room and over to the fireplace mantle that's decorated with pictures of my best friend and me.

I feel my brain suddenly kick back into gear as I register what she just said.

"She died yesterday, when?" I tense and wait for her answer. My best friend could have been dead for twenty-four hours and I've been sitting here reading calculus textbooks none the wiser. I'm so mad but I don't know where to place my anger, at my math teacher for giving out extra homework, at the Wilson's for not calling me and letting me know it was time, or at myself. I should have visited her yesterday like I was supposed to. Now it's too late.

"It was just before midnight, she went peacefully and she wouldn't have been in any pain."

I hadn't even thought about that. I take a deep breath and feel my shoulders relax a little.

"She's dead," I say to myself, and then look up into Nurse Carla's eyes. They're filled with unshed tears. I'm sure this isn't the first time she's had to deliver this kind of news, but I don't suppose it gets any easier.

I can hear the next-door neighbor's little girls playing in the yard. They remind me of Emily and me, They're always laughing, and normally it makes me smile, but today I want to shout at them to stop. There's no reason to laugh right now, no reason to smile. For them it's just another day. Not for me, though. I know with absolute certainty that whenever I look back on today, I'll be reminded of the loss of my best friend. It will all be tucked away neatly in my mind, every last excruciating detail.

"Sweetie, is your mom at work? Should I call her, so she can come be with you?"

I drop my head and squeeze my eyes tight, hoping to stop the steady flow of tears that seem to be escaping despite my best efforts.

"No, I'm fine. There's no need to call her. I'm eighteen, not twelve, it's not like I wasn't expecting Emily to die, I knew it was coming."

"Just because you were expecting it, Blair, doesn't mean that it won't still affect you. She was your best friend." She sighs and carries on. "I told Emily's mom that I would come and tell you. The Wilson's are obviously very upset, but Pam wanted me to give you this."

She holds out a pink envelope, with 'Blair' scribbled across the front in purple ink, a heart dotting the I in my name. It's Emily's handwriting; if the heart didn't give it away, the purple ink would have. She only wrote in purple—I'm not sure that I ever asked her why, and now I can't.

I take the envelope from Nurse Carla and thank her

for dropping by to tell me. It feels kind of ironic to thank someone for just breaking your heart. I really need her to leave so that I can process what's happened. She attempts to give me an awkward hug and then sees herself out. I watch her wave from the car as she pulls out of my drive, I'm still frozen to the spot at the fireplace, watching her through the window, sure that my heart will shatter if I move.

Blair

Three Months Later

I SIT STARING at the unopened envelope pinned onto my notice board above the desk in my room. It's filled with pictures of Emily and me through the years. There are pictures of us from grade school with braces and no front teeth; pictures of us at the mall in one of those photo booths, pulling stupid faces and giving our best pout; stalker pictures of Emily in the halls by Ethan Jamison's locker, Ethan in the background having no idea we were trying to take pictures of him. I lean back in my desk chair and crack my knuckles, stretching out my arms above my head. I'm going to do it. The thought makes me feel sick and dizzy, I can feel my eyes start to prick with tears. I let out a sigh.

"Get a freaking grip, Blair, it's just a letter," I say aloud.

I unpin it from the board, shaking so much that my name in all its purple ink glory is blurring into the pink of

4

the envelope. I want to read it. I need to read it. It's been haunting me for the past three goddamn months. Only I know, once I finally do open it, that's it. That's the last thing I'll ever have from Emily. I know I need to just do it, but it hurts, it hurts so damn much that I want to scream.

I take a calming breath, roll my shoulders and carefully open the envelope and pull the letter out, sending a ton of pink glitter and purple heart confetti soaring into the air. It rains down over me, covering my desk and bedroom floor. I'm gonna be sparkly for a month. I hate glitter. Emily knew that, it's no oversight. The thought makes me smile; she knew she'd be pissing me off. I unfold the paper and stare down at her handwriting, attempting to focus on the words.

Blair,

If you're reading this then I've obviously croaked it. Lol! I know it's not funny but I kinda have to make a joke of it, so that what I'm writing doesn't feel so real, you know? I'm writing this letter to you after just finishing the one I've written for my mom and dad. I need to lighten the mood, so I'm gonna confess something. I can say it now because I'm not here anymore and there'll be no retaliation. It's a cheap trick, but you know you love me.

Last year when Corey Spencer asked you out, and then cancelled on you at the last minute, I may or may not have accidentally told him that you used to write Mrs. Blair Spencer and practice your signature at the back of your journal.

And I may have also told him that you had your kids' names picked out already. I know, I know, I totally freaked him out! I thought he'd laugh and tease you about it on your date, but I guess he kinda thought you were a bunny boiler and bailed. Sorry!!!

Okay, so now that I have that off my chest, I need you to do something for me and you can't say no, because it's a dying girl's wish! Yeah, I know, I played the dying BFF card. But please, just think about it.

So, I have a bucket list. Totally morbid and cliché, but never mind. Last year when I was told the cancer wasn't going away I listed all the things that I wanted to do before I take my Long Sleep. I didn't tell you or Mom because I wanted something that was just mine, that I'd achieved, and I managed to cross a few of them off. You were actually with me for most of them, but not all of them, and that's where I need your help.

I figured that there has to be something after this life, right? This can't just be it; at least I hope this isn't just it. If there is such a thing as reincarnation and I can still visit you or see you from my cloud (yep, I'm totes gonna spend my days laying out on clouds), then if you finish my list it would be like me getting to experience it. I know it sounds crazy but hear me out. You're the closet person to me. My mom always says we're practically the same girl with different hair. And if it were the other way around, I would do this for you. I'd complain and bitch about it, but I would still do it.

My list is attached. I know what I'm asking is probably unfair, but you know how I hate not finishing something I started, be it homework or cheesecake. Lol! So, #10 is a ridiculous ask—you really don't have to do that—but a kiss would suffice. :-) I really wish I'd made a play for that hot piece of ass.

Anyway, if you decide you can't, don't worry, I won't haunt you. I love you more than the stars.

You're the most awesome friend a girl could ever have wished for. I have so many awesome memories and every one of them includes you. You have been my shoulder to cry on, my punching bag, literally and verbally. You made me feel happy when I didn't think there was anything to be happy about, and I'm gonna miss you the most. You're like the other half of me, the Bert to my Ernie, the peanut butter to my jelly!!!

I love you, Blair. I always will.

Emily xoxo

P.S. You would have totally been my maid of honor when I finally married Ethan Jamison and had a billion of his sexy ass babies.

The List

1. ~~Swim with dolphins~~
2. Visit the Grand Canyon
3. Go to Vegas, baby!
4. Sing/Perform for a crowd
5. ~~Tell Mr. Parker he's a dick!~~
6. Skinny dip
7. Get completely wasted
8. ~~Smoke a cigarette~~
9. Fall in love
10. Lose my V card (Ideally Ethan Jamison!)
11. ~~Sleep under the stars~~
12. ~~Ride a horse~~
13. ~~Volunteer (hospital/old folks' home/ homeless shelter)~~
14. ~~TP Harriet Clare's house~~

15. Ride in a hot air balloon
16. Visit Paris
17. Get a tattoo
18. Send a message in a bottle
19. Dye my hair bright pink
20. Try Surfing

I feel my cell vibrate and I don't have to look at the screen to know it's Mom. The only other person who ever called was Emily. I don't have many friends, or ones who call me, anyway. Emily and I were practically joined at the hip; she was the cool, outgoing one and I was the shy, awkward one.

She was the person everyone gravitated towards, drawing people in like moths to a flame. You couldn't help but notice her light. Since she's been gone, Casey and Brie have made several attempts to get me to hang out but it just feels too weird without Emily being there as my buffer. They were always more her friends than mine. We have zero in common without Emily.

"Hey," I answer.

"Hi, honey, I'm on my way home from the office now, dropping by the store. Is there anything you need me to pick up?"

She sounds entirely too freaking happy for my mood at the moment.

"No Mom, I'm good, I'm just studying, so I'll see you when you get back." My voice sounds all scratchy from crying and I know she'll call me out on it, so I press end on the call before she gets a chance.

That leaves me about forty minutes to get my shit together before she's home. I quickly fold the letter and put it in my desk drawer before heading to the bathroom to wash my face, and hopefully gain some perspective on what the hell I just read.

elle

I can hear pots and pans banging in the kitchen as I step out of the shower, which means Mom must be making dinner. I'm starving and right on cue my stomach rumbles. I head to my room, dry off and pull on a pair of yoga pants and my bright green t-shirt that says '*Mathletes*' across the chest. I study myself in the mirror; my long brown hair is a matted wet mess that's soaking the back of my shirt so I quickly tie it in a messy bun on top of my head. I'm slim and relatively short. Five feet five inches actually, which isn't tiny, but considering my mom's five eleven and my dad was six two, you'd think I'd be taller.

I used to think that maybe I was adopted, but then as I got older, I started to really look like my mom, minus the height. We are both ridiculously pale skinned, with dark brown hair and the same big almond-shaped green eyes, although mine are always hidden beneath my glasses. I have contacts but prefer to wear glasses; poking myself in the eye every day to put in and take out contacts is a pain in the ass.

Mom shouts up that dinner's ready and I make my way downstairs to say hello. I walk into the kitchen and she's sitting at the island, two plates of mac and cheese and a half drunk bottle of wine in front of her. There was none open when I came down to get a drink earlier, and she's only been home about twenty minutes. Guess she's on a mission to get wasted. Don't get me wrong—she's a good mom, but since dad died about three years ago, there's not many nights that she's not half cut. I make a point of not talking about it, and she's happy to ignore the fact that she's not gonna find the answer to her problems at the bottom of a bottle. It's a pretty messed-up situation. We can talk about almost anything else, just not that. Emily was the only person I ever used to talk to about it. Hell, I miss her.

Chapter 2

Ethan

"HERE, TRY THIS, it'll help," my mom says, passing me an ice pack for my jaw. When dad saw my report card and noticed I wasn't pulling straight A's he was more than a little pissed at me.

"He's under a lot of pressure at work, sweetheart; you know that. He has high expectations for you about college, Ethan."

Yet again she's making excuses for him; it's her forte. She can't look me in the eye while she says it, though. I knew he'd be pissed at me for failing math, but I was still stupid enough to mutter under my breath that it was 'my life'. He heard that and lost his shit real quick. He doesn't normally hit me in the face because it draws attention. I normally get beaten where the bruises can be hidden. I could fight back, I'm big enough to take him, but I don't. I just stand there completely numb and take it. I'm pretty sure it would kill my mom to see us beating the shit out of each other. So, I suck it up and tell myself I'll be out of here soon.

ele

I pull my car into my usual spot in the school lot and check the rearview mirror to inspect the bruise that's starting to form across my jaw. I notice Jackson and TJ making their way over to my Camaro. I sigh and grab my backpack from the passenger seat; I could really do without school today.

"Yo Ethan my man, where the hell have you been all weekend?" TJ hollers, coming to a standstill beside my car.

"Dude, what the hell happened to your face?" Jackson cuts in.

I shoot him a look that says 'shut the fuck up', and then shrug and tell them I was hit in the face while shooting hoops. TJ looks like he buys it but Jackson's been my best friend since kindergarten. He knows my dad's a prick, and I'm pretty sure he's put two and two together over the years. But he also knows not to ask me about it. I grab my jacket from the backseat, slam the car door closed, and we make our way across the parking lot and head into school with the usual group of girls clamoring around us. There are definite perks to being in a band, but having girls constantly trying to claim the title of girlfriend gets old fast. It seems the less interested I am, the more interested they become.

"Hey, Ethan," Brie says, coming to stand next to my locker.

Brie's hot but she knows it and it's a total turn off, she's your stereotypical head cheerleader-—blonde hair, long legs and lip-gloss. I'd tell her to take a hike, but she's wearing a tiny excuse of a shirt with her boobs pushed up on display, and I'm a guy, after all.

"Hey, what's up?" I say to her tits rather than to her face.

"I hear you're having trouble in professor Hillman's class, and I just wanted to let you know I'm totally available if you need help studying." She says this in a whiney voice that I'm assuming she means to be sexy, while running her hand down my arm. I shrug away from her reach and lift my gaze from her tits to answer her.

"Thanks for the offer, Brie, but I'm pretty sure we wouldn't get much studying done." I wink and push off my locker, heading down the hall before she has time to reply. Jackson jogs up beside me, laughing.

"Dude, what's wrong with you? Why the hell aren't you tapping that?"

"I've seen her outside my house a few times, I think she follows me," I say shrugging. "Plus her voice is like a cheese grater to me, man, and I bet she's a screamer." I laugh as we head to first period.

$$\mathcal{ele}$$

I walk into the cafeteria to grab lunch; I'm late because Hillman held me back to tell me that I'm fucking useless at math. He gave me the number of some nerd I'm supposed to call about tutoring. Apparently she's agreed to help me for extra credit or some shit, I don't know. It's gonna be awkward as hell. I grab a sandwich and bottle of water and head over to sit with the guys.

It's your typical high school clique seating plan: the Emos and Goths sit at the far back corner of the cafeteria, looking…well, depressed; the Nerds and Band Geeks sit a little ways in front of them; then it's your average students that just want to fit in; then the Jocks and Cheerleaders, and then us. I sit with the rest of the members of our band, Kickstart. It just happens that Jackson is also a jock, volleyball player by day, drummer by night. Our table usually has a weird mix of musicians and jocks.

"Dude, move over." I push Jackson along the bench seat so I can sit at the end of the table.

"What did Hillman want, E?"

I look over to Drew, ready to reply, but he's already lost focus and is now pulling his girlfriend Dannii on his lap, burying his head into her neck. Drew's a good-looking kid, but it's taken a while for him to grow into those looks. Dannii is hot and knows it. He thinks he's punching above his weight, even though since we've started playing more gigs he has girls throwing themselves at him. If you ask me, it's the other way around: Dannii is the one punching above her weight. Drew's a great guy.

"Yo, get a room!" TJ shouts and then whips his head back in my direction. "Yeah man, what did Hillman want?"

"He gave me a number to organize some tutoring, says I need to bring my grades up or he's failing me."

"How you gonna fit that in with practice? Steve will shit a brick if you start missing them!"

I sigh and talk around a huge chunk of sandwich.

"Gonna have to squeeze it in on a week night, I

16

guess."

"Sucks to be you, man," Jackson pipes in.

Yeah, it really does fucking suck to be me. I pull out my cell and tap out a message to the number Professor Hillman gave me.

To: Tutor Nerd
Hi,
Professor Hillman gave me your number to contact you about math tutoring.
Ethan.

I slide the cell back into my pocket and pick up my shit and make to leave; I'm beyond annoyed at myself for dropping grades in math. It should be second nature since I play the piano and read sheet music; most people don't realize the math involved in that. I guess I was taking for granted that I've always been good at it. I'm tired and my jaw still hurts like hell. I am so done with this shitty day.

"I'm heading over to the music department, you guys coming?" I'm looking back to the table. Jackson, TJ and Drew all stand and start to gather their crap, Drew kisses Dannii goodbye and the rest of us just roll our eyes. PDA's are for pussies. They've been together for about a month and I'm pretty sure that if Dannii ate a cookie, Drew could spit that fucker up, they're that close already. She has him wrapped around her little finger and everyone sees it but him.

"Later, guys!" she shouts before planting one last kiss on Drew and whispering something to him before we leave.

Chapter 3

Blair

MY CELL VIBRATES and I pull it from my jacket and stare down at the screen. The display shows one new text from a number I don't recognize. I'm a little confused about who would be texting until I remember that I gave my contact details to Professor Hillman. Some guy in one of his classes is flunking and he's agreed to give me extra credit if I can get this kid's grades up. I don't really need the credit but he's also said he'll write me a letter of recommendation to go with my application to Cornell.

The guy hasn't put his last name on the text and I know of at least four Ethans off the top of my head. I shoot back a text.

To: Ethan
Hi, my name's Blair Thomas. I'm available tonight if you want to make a start straight away. I will be in the school library from 4pm.

I go to put my cell back in my pocket when a response comes through.

From: Ethan
Hi Blair,
I can't make it till 4:30 - is that ok? Should I meet you at the entrance to the library and how do I know who to look for?
Ethan

I read the text and have to resist like hell telling him I'll be the girl reading a newspaper in a red sweater, holding a rose like they do in all the cheesy rom-coms. That would probably freak him out. Most people don't get my humor. Emily did, the thought makes me frown.

To: Ethan
Ethan,
4:30 is fine, just come straight into the library; I'll most likely be the only student in there. You won't miss me.
B

I put the cell back in my pocket and make my way from the quad where I was eating lunch, through the cafeteria and back towards my locker.

"Blair, hold up!" Casey shouts as she and Brie make their way towards me.

They kind of look like your typical high school Barbie dolls, except they're actually pretty cool, and surprisingly smart for cheerleaders. Cheap blow but undeniably true. The rest of the cheer squad couldn't muster up a brain cell between them.

"Girl, where have you been? I've been looking for you since second period. I've got your notes from Lit class that I borrowed," Casey says thrusting my notepad at me.

Casey's funny as hell; she's the epitome of a country club princess, her family is posh but she talks with no filter and is pretty loud and all up in your face—finger snapping and head whipping from side to side. Half the time I actually wonder if she's high.

"Thanks Case, I wa—" I'm cut off before I can finish my sentence by Brie hopping up and down on the spot like an over excited puppy, her blonde hair and boobs bouncing all over the place.

"Ooh Blair, you coming to TJ's party Friday night? Everyone's going, and the volleyball team will be there, and so will Kickstart," she says, wiggling her eyebrows with a huge grin on her face.

"Yeah, you should, totally come with us. I'm driving over at about 8:00 and I can pick you up on the way," Case cuts in.

It's common knowledge that those parties are supposed to be pretty full on. Part of me wants to go, just to experience it for myself. Plus Kickstart is supposedly awesome. Em told me that Ethan Jamison writes most of their music and is stupidly talented. She *would* think that, though.

"Thanks guys, but it's not really my scene. Plus, I don't really know anyone from the volleyball team so it would be kinda awkward."

"You know everyone on the volleyball team. Don't feed us that crap; I haven't seen you outside school since

Emily died. Please come with us, don't be such a bore."
Brie flashes me her best sad puppy dog eyes. I actually
contemplate it for about a nanosecond before coming back
to my senses.

"Sorry guys, I can't. It's not my scene and for the
record, Brie, knowing who everyone is on the volleyball
team isn't the same as actually knowing them enough to
talk to them. Plus, if Kickstart is there the place will already be over crowded. I have to go, I'm um…I'm late for
my next class," I say, walking away from their pouts as
quickly as I can without actually running.

ele

I look down at my cell and it's 4:54pm. No sign of
Ethan. No text to explain. What a douche. I mean, okay so
I needed to be here anyway to collect books, but that's not
the point. He didn't know that. I can't stand people that
make plans and then break them without warning. It takes
two seconds to send a text.

I'm packing up my things when Ethan Jamison barges
through the library doors. He's panting like he's out of
breath and his eyes are frantically scanning the almost
empty room. Then they land on me. I stand completely
frozen, mouth gaping like a total moron. Of freaking
course it has to be that Ethan. He makes his way over, and
the sound of his boots echoing through the otherwise silent
room awakens me from my dumbstruck state. Emily's letter flashes in my mind and I feel instantly embarrassed.
Like, somehow he knows about it, which of course, he
can't, but I'm still panicking.

He stops a few feet short of my table and looks a little unsure. This isn't the cocky Ethan Jamison that struts around school thinking he's god's gift. It's thrown me a little.

"Hey, um…I'm Ethan," he says, looking down at me. He lays his guitar case down at his feet and then adjusts his backpack on his shoulders. "Are you the tutor, I mean, sorry…are you Blair?"

I never realized how tall he actually is up close and personal. I've seen him play at a gig for about two seconds once, but he was on a stage, so of course he's gonna look taller than everyone else. Emily and I have only stalked him at a distance. His blue eyes are boring into mine and I'm just standing there. Staring. Like an idiot. He shifts his weight and I realize he's asked me a question. I still haven't replied. Shit.

"Er…yeah, I'm Blair, nice to meet you. I was just about to go, I thought you weren't coming. You're late." The last part comes out all pissy like I'm mad at him.

An amused grin starts to form; his mouth pulling up slightly at one side and the boy has dimples—real life honest-to-god dimples.

I shake my head and practically bark out, "I've been waiting for you for almost a half hour. If you're gonna be late when we meet, you could at least give me a heads up?" Oh my god, why the hell am I telling him off?

His smile widens and he's not even *trying* to look sorry. He drops his backpack on the table and takes a seat.

"Yeah, I had practice and it ran over. Steve has a no phone rule, so it's kinda hard to let you know when I don't have my cell."

Steve is the music professor; he's got the new age

hippy vibe going on and makes all his students call him by his first name. I pull my chair back out and take a seat. "Okay. Well, um, let's just get started then."

I look up and his eyes are zeroed in on my chest. What a complete douche, he's already ogling my boobs. I cough twice and raise my eyebrows in a 'what the hell, my eyes are up here' stare, and his cheeks immediately redden.

"Shit, no, I wasn't checking you out! I mean…um, I wasn't staring at your…fuck, well I kinda was but I mean, shit; I was just trying to read what your shirt says."

Holy crap, this guy's more awkward than I am. I laugh but it comes out more of a snort, not my most attractive feature.

"It says 'come to the nerd side we have pi'. You know, pi as in the math term, that's what the symbol represents."

He's just staring at me now and it's my turn to feel all kinds of awkward. He breaks the silence by full-out laughing.

"I know I need a math tutor, Blair…but I know what the symbol for pi looks like. I'm actually not bad at math, I've just let it slip."

I can't help but laugh too. I'm pretty sure he's laughing at me rather than with me, but it's breaking the tension, so what the heck.

"Oh, well okay, so yeah, slogan tees are kind of my thing," I say whilst trying to compose myself.

As first impressions go, I don't think this could have gone much worse. He probably thinks I am a giant geek and he wouldn't be far wrong. If Emily could witness this exchange, she would be in hysterics. I basically shout at the hottest guy in school for being late, accuse him of staring at my boobs, and then proceed to talk to him like a five-year-old and explain pi. Kill. Me. Now!

ele

We've been in the library almost two hours and I'm absolutely starving. As if on cue, Ethan closes his textbook and leans back in his seat, stretching his arms above his head. I watch as the muscles in his chest and arms tense and suddenly, it's not just food I'm hungry for. Ethan Jamison is HOT. I never really allowed myself to pay much attention to him. Emily crushed on him from the first day of school and called dibs, so I've never really given him a second thought. She used to make me take pictures of her while he was somewhere in the background and silly shit like that, but he was always her obsession, not mine. Sure, I knew he was good looking, I'm not blind or a lesbian, but hell, I should have paid more attention.

His brown hair is sticking up in all directions from running his hands through it while I was trying to explain a formula to him. He's got that surfer boy golden skin, like he spends all of his free time outside. His black Henley is pulled tight over his chest and now I'm the one caught staring.

"Wanna go and get something to eat? I'm starving."

"Huh? Oh, um…yeah, I was just thinking about how hungry I was."

He smiles back full force because he knows I just checked him out and was staring at his chest. He pushes back from the table and stands, putting his books back into his bag.

"I know a great pizza place about ten minutes away, how about it?" He swings the backpack over his shoulder, picks his guitar case up and stands looking down at me, waiting for an answer.

I'm packing my books away and stop. The shock is probably evident on my face, Ethan Jamison just asked me to go get something to eat with him. Wait, does this count as a date? What the hell ever. There's only one place I'm heading right now.

"Count me in. I'll go get my car and follow you there. Or wait…do you need a ride?"

"No, I'm good, my car's in the lot." He turns to leave and I'm following behind, trying my best to not drool as I watch his ass. I'm using all my restraint right now to stop myself from doing a happy dance.

Chapter 4

Ethan

I'M AT A stoplight and Blair is following behind in her car. I'm looking in the rear view mirror and I can just about make out her face. She's singing along to music, throwing her head back and forth and from what I can see, she's really going for it. I can't help but watch, it's pretty fucking funny.

I hear a car honk and realize that the lights have changed and I'm still sitting here like a creeper watching her. I put my foot down and head towards Marco's Pizzeria. It's been bugging me since I walked in the library and saw her—why don't I know who she is? I pretty much know every senior in the school. As soon as I climbed in my car, I texted Jackson asking who she was and if he knew her. I still haven't had a reply. Asshole.

I've pulled up and we're walking into the restaurant when my cell finally beeps with a new message from Jackson;

From: Jackson

Dude, Brie's friend Emily Wilson, the girl that died of cancer? She's her friend — sometimes hangs with Brie and Casey. Why? She your tutor? Corey reckons the chick's a Stage 5 clinger. Lol!

I'm walking and not paying attention to anything but my cell when I slam straight into the back of Blair who's stopped walking. She's standing at the entrance by the 'Please Wait to be Seated' sign and the force of my impact makes her stumble forward, so I throw my arms out to catch her by the waist and drop my cell in the process.

"Shit, sorry…you okay? I didn't see you stop."

"I'm fine, no worries."

I stand holding her waist and we just stare at each other until suddenly she shrugs away from my grasp, picks up my phone and passes it back to me.

I glance back down at the text from Jackson and hope she hasn't seen it. She's looking at me strangely. I shrug and try to school my confusion as to how Corey knows this chick. I don't know why, but it bothers me.

"Is everything okay?" she asks in a concerned voice.

"Yeah, my friend, Jackson was just replying to a text I'd sent him."

"If you had other plans we can just forget this, I don't mind."

"No, not at all, don't be dumb. I wouldn't bring you here and then just bail. I'm not a total dick."

"Just a little bit of one, huh?" she says, smiling.

"Wow, now you've gone and hurt my feelings," I say, mock pouting and clutching my chest.

"I'm sure you'll get over it."

I'm dying to tell her I'd rather get under it but don't. "I'm actually a really sensitive guy." I wink, turn my cell onto vibrate and put it back in my pocket.

"You been to this place before? I must eat here at least once a week. They have the best meatball pizzas on the planet."

She scrunches her nose up and shakes her head no. "I'm not a meatball fan, they make me think of dog food," she says as she bites her lip.

She looks up at me through the black-rimmed hipster glasses she's wearing; I'm too busy staring at her lips to realize that she's still talking to me. Now I have no clue what she just said. Awkward.

The whole time we were in the library I was tripping over my tongue like a complete loser. I was fine until the whole staring at her tits and pi explanation, then I just lost it. I started nervous laughing and then she snorted. By that point I was laughing my ass off. Since then all I've been doing is trying to think of something clever or funny to say.

The normal Ethan Jamison definitely won't cut it, her shirt alone lets me know that she doesn't give a shit what other people think of her. She doesn't take herself too seriously. She's different from all the other girls I know and it's intriguing. She clears her throat and I realize that I've spaced out again. Christ, she's gonna think I'm retarded.

I've finished my pizza and she's about halfway through hers and up to this point the conversation's been pretty standard. Although, when I talk to her, she has a way of making me feel like she's really listening to me. I've managed to hold my own without making a jackass out of myself for a full thirty minutes now. This new Ethan I seem to have morphed into is pretty pleased with himself. The old Ethan would want to kick this new one's ass. I normally don't have to try at all with girls. They seem to like the whole musician package I have going on. This girl, on the other hand, couldn't seem less impressed with that if she tried. It's refreshing.

She's still eating and I can't take my eyes off her mouth. At first glance, Blair is good looking—nothing special—but up close you can see she has the most amazing huge green eyes and I wonder what she looks like with her glasses off. She has the sexiest mouth I think I've ever seen. I shake my head to remove the inappropriate thoughts assaulting my mind of what I want to do to that mouth, or rather what I want that mouth to be doing to me. I clear my throat.

"So what music are you into?" I ask, hoping to keep the conversation going. I'm running out of things to say and I don't want to have to struggle to fill the silence. If there's one thing I can talk forever about, it's music.

"I guess I have eclectic taste. I like a little of everything. You know, Rihanna, The Civil Wars, John Legend, The Avett Brothers, The Stones…anything, really. My iPod's a giant mess of songs."

I smile inwardly at myself that she didn't just answer pop. "Cool. So, um, what where you listening to on the way here?"

Her eyebrows draw together and she cocks her head to the side, "BonJovi, I think, why?"

I huff out a laugh; I didn't have her pegged as liking classic rock. "I was watching you sing in your car; man, you were really going for it."

I instantly regret bringing it up, her face has fallen and her cheeks have colored. I'm pretty sure mine match, since I've just admitted that I was staring at her like a creeper.

"Oh god, I'm so embarrassed! Oh, well, I suppose at least you couldn't hear me, right?"

"Don't worry, it was equal parts funny and cute."

"Really? Well, you gotta love BonJovi."

She's smiling now and it's doing something to me. I guess it's because she can tell she's not the only one embarrassed. Either way, I don't really care. I could watch this girl smile all damn day. I take a sip of my water and try think of something that will keep her smiling, because apparently the new me has developed ovaries. I almost want to run my hands over my chest to make sure I haven't sprouted a pair of double D's to match. In a couple of hours I've gone from confident musician to the kind of douche I'd normally laugh at with the guys. Holy shit, that's a scary thought!

I'm tempted to ask her out on a date, but I have practice every night this week and Dad finding out I blew it off for a date just isn't worth it. The thought of him makes me tense and I have to concentrate on trying to relax my shoulders.

"So, I should really be getting back," she tells me, as she pulls her napkin from her lap and bunches it up on the table.

"No problem." Our eyes lock and when they do it feels like she can see straight through to my soul. Past all the macho bullshit. Past the cocky player. I feel like she knows all my secrets and yet she just sees me. The thought is fucking terrifying.

She leans in closer and for one second I think she's actually making to kiss me, and then she raises her hand and brushes her fingers across my jaw.

"What happened?"

I feel lightheaded, she's so close. Her eyes widen as she realizes that she's touching me and pulls her hand back quickly, looking shocked at herself.

I want her hands back on me. Then I register that she's asking about my jaw and I instantly tense.

"Oh, nothing…I took an elbow to the face shooting hoops." I shrug, hoping she doesn't question it further.

She's staring at me with a look in her eyes that says she doesn't believe me, but she's not about to call me out on it. The tension's starting to suffocate me and I need to change the subject. This girl makes me want to tell her the truth and I've only known her for about ten seconds.

"You free to study again Friday after practice?" I ask, noticing she's starting to fidget with the sleeves of her jacket.

"Don't have any plans, huh? I thought you'd be going to the party Friday night, aren't you playing?"

"Oh, yeah that. I'd forgotten about that, I'm supposed to be going…doesn't matter if I turn up late, though, I am the star." I meant it jokingly but out loud it just makes me sound like a prick. I want to ask her to come with me, but I'm pretty sure that she would say no and I don't want this girl to reject me.

"Yeah, okay then, I'm free. Same time in the library?"

"How about you come to my place after I'm done with my practice? That way I can head to TJ's as soon as we're done."

"It's a date," she says, then her cheeks burn bright red and she stammers, "No I didn't mean it's a date, date. Just that it's a date, like we've set a date. Oh my god, I mean I'll be there…ugh, whatever, you know what I mean."

I can't help the ridiculous grin on my face. This girl is too cute.

"Relax, I know what you meant. I'll text you my address, yeah?" I motion over to the waitress to bring the check.

We leave the restaurant and she doesn't look back at me once as she gets into her car and pulls away. My eyes are trained on her until the car disappears. The whole way home all I can think about is how much it bothered me that she left without looking back. I don't like watching her leave and yet I can't work out the hell why.

I turn onto my street and remember promising I'd be home straight after practice to help Dad move some furniture into the garage. Fuck. Shit. Fuck.

Excuses are running through my head, rather than telling him the truth. If there's one thing he won't tolerate it's people breaking plans. He's almost to the point of O.C.D about following through with arrangements. It's all about discipline and structure. It's the cop in him, he expects everyone to practice what he preaches. His word is law. He's been on the force my whole life. Roughly the same amount of time he's been an asshole. I see him standing at the garage as I'm pulling into the driveway. He's looking all kinds of pissed. Ice cold dread seeps through my veins as I pull to a stop and climb out of my car. His eyes lock with mine and now I know I'm screwed.

Chapter 5

Blair

"WHERE'VE YOU BEEN? I've been worried sick!" Mom practically shouts as I walk through the front door. I kick my shoes off in the hall and make my way through to the kitchen and get myself a soda.

"Blair did you hear me, where have you been?"

"I told you I was going to be late getting home; I was tutoring. We finished and got hungry so we stopped and had dinner—what's the problem?" I know my tone is pissy, but she's sitting at the kitchen island looking annoyed and I don't want her to bring me down off my Ethan-induced high.

"I didn't get your text," she says in an accusatory manner, and I know she's not in the best mood. She looks tired and she's always in a foul mood when she's tired. I sigh and lean on my elbows across the island.

"I texted you a couple of hours ago, Mom. How's your day been?"

"Same as usual—Clare's off sick so it's been busy but nothing new. So, who are you tutoring?"

I take a long drink of the soda I've just taken from the fridge and then look at Mom eying me curiously. I know she knows who Ethan Jamison is, the whole town does. Emily used to talk about him non-stop, too, and she's seen the stalker pics pinned to my notice board. She laughed her ass off when Emily told her that she'd made me take pictures of her with Ethan in the background. Told us that we were heading the right way for a restraining order.

"It's Ethan Jamison," I answer, trying to be nonchalant and portray zero emotion in my voice. Her head snaps back up from her coffee and there's a smile forming across her face. All traces of her shitty mood gone.

"Emily's Ethan?"

"He was never really Emily's Ethan, Mom, but yeah, that Ethan." *Please drop it, please drop it.*

"No, but you knew who I meant. Is he as cute in real life as he is in his pictures?"

I snort and send soda spraying all over the island. Mom looks at me wide-eyed for a second before bursting out laughing. I can't help but join her; I have soda dripping from my chin and a slight burning sensation at the back of my nose from the fizz. I suddenly realize that I can't recall the last time we laughed like this, it's been so long and the thought saddens me. I wipe at my face with my sleeve and answer her.

"He's actually better looking in person. He's having trouble in Professor Hillman's class. I get extra credit for helping him."

Mom looks over at me and wiggles her eyebrows. "It's a win, win then."

I smile and nod. "Definitely."

Mom picks her coffee mug back up and motions for me to follow her into the living room.

"Come and tell me more about Ethan, honey."

"There's nothing to tell, really. This is the first I've ever really spoken to him. I'm helping him study again Friday night. It's weird; he's kind of funny and totally not how I expected him to be at all. At school he walks the halls like he owns them, but today he was different. I don't know, we sort of got off on the wrong foot but it helped, I think."

"What do you mean you got off on the wrong foot?" she says sitting on the sofa and drawing her legs up underneath her.

"Honestly, it was so cringe-worthy and stupid it doesn't even matter. But I guess it broke the ice. If he'd turned up and acted like I was expecting him to, like 'I'm so cool I'm in a band worship me', I don't think we'd have ended up going for dinner or even getting along at all."

"Really…so you like him, huh?"

"What? No, that's not what I mean. He was just nicer than I was expecting is all. I don't *like him* like him."

"Uh-huh…that's not what that smile's telling me, baby girl. Don't kid a kidder, Blair."

I can't help but smile wider. Busted.

ele

I'm cranky as hell as I make my way to first period. I got next to no sleep last night. After the initial Ethan high wore off, I was consumed with a feeling of guilt that I was crushing on Emily's Ethan. I took her letter out of my desk and read it over and over until I couldn't see anything through my tears. I must have fallen asleep from the sheer exhaustion of crying.

I woke late this morning with puffy eyes and a split-ting headache. I did decide one thing in my hormonally-induced girly meltdown. I need to suck it up and cross the things off her list. She's asked me to do one thing, and if I can't do that, then what kind of a friend does that make me? I know without a doubt she would do the same for me, although I can't ever imagine asking her to. Maybe if I can do this for her it will give me closure. I still can't wrap my head around the fact that she is actually gone. It's been months, and I still find myself waiting for her phone calls. I miss her so much.

I contemplated ditching but then I gave myself a 'quit it with the pity' pep talk and hauled ass to school. Now I'm making my way through the halls and I can't help but scan them for any sign of Ethan. I know I shouldn't but I can't help myself. He's gotten under my skin and it's more than a little unsettling.

I quickly come to the conclusion that he's not here today. I've seen most of the guys from the volleyball team and all the other members of Kickstart at one point or an-other, but he's nowhere to be found. He wasn't at the douche table at lunch, either. The amount of time Ethan Jamison has consumed my mind today is ridiculous; I kind of want to kick my own ass for being such a girl. I need to get a grip. This isn't me.

I catch my reflection as I pass the windows in the hall on the way to my locker. I pulled my hair into a low pony-tail this morning and I run my hand through it, pausing as a memory of Emily assaults my mind. I'm instantly transported back to the week after her diagnosis. Mom had taken me to UCLA Health Center to visit her. Pam had called my mom and told her she was having a rough day; her hair had started to fall out when she'd taken a shower and it had freaked her out.

When we arrived at the hospital, Pam, my mom and Bill, Em's dad had left us to go grab a coffee. Emily was sitting hugging her knees resting against the headboard of the hospital bed. She was so pale it almost didn't look like her. I can see the scene perfectly in my mind now.

"It's happening already, Blair, I didn't think it would be this fast. I've only been on chemo a week and my hair is falling out in clumps every time I touch it."

I sat down on the bed beside her and rubbed my hand in small circles over her back.

"You'll still be beautiful with no hair, you know. And it will grow back super fast, you can rock one of those pixie haircuts all the stars go for."

"I do have great cheek bones." She half smiled.

"Exactly! You'll look freaking amazing."

She looked back at me and I expected a smart quip, but instead I was met with a weak smile that quickly morphed into a look of utter sadness as her eyes welled and she let out a sob. I reached over and pulled her to me, enveloping her in a tight hug.

"I'm going to look like a real cancer patient now," she sniffed. *"Everyone will stare at me."*

"Hey, it's just hair, Em. You know what? If people stare at you, they'll have to stare at me, too." I shuffled

back off the bed. "I'll be back in a sec."

I found a nurse at the desk out in the hall and asked her to help me with something. Five minutes later I was followed back into Emily's room by a nurse whose name tag read, 'Jolly'. She was an older woman with spiky purple hair and rosy cheeks.

"Hello Emily, Blair asked me to come in and help her with something," Jolly announced.

Em shot me a confused look and I grinned and pulled the chair from the corner of the room out into the middle and sat down. I pulled my ponytail over my shoulder and before Em could register what was about to happen, I took the scissors that Jolly had given me, and sliced straight through my long brown hair. I was left with my ponytail in my hand as my remaining hair sprang up and fell over my face, into my eyes.

"Oh my god! No! Blair, what are you doing?" she gasped.

"Like I said, if anyone stares now, it will be at the two of us, not just you."

Tears spilled down her cheeks as she rushed over to hug me.

"I love you, Blair."

"I love you, too, now let me go. You're crushing me, I can't breathe," I laughed. "Jolly, do your stuff." I said, as Nurse Jolly plugged a shaver into the wall socket. It took less than five minutes before I looked like I was about to enlist in the army. My buzzed head felt bumpy and way colder than I expected it to.

"Okay, you next." I motioned to Em and she traded places with me and sat down on the chair. "Let's get you shaved, too. This way you don't have to get upset every

time a piece falls out."

"Our moms are going to freak!" she answered with wide eyes.

"Let them." I laughed.

Our parents walked through the door just as Nurse Jolly swept up the last of the hair and dumped it into a trash bag to take out of the room. I looked to the door where Pam immediately burst into tears and rushed forward, kissing Emily on the forehead before scooping her up and holding her tight to her chest. Bill's eyes glazed over as he slowly made his way across the room and enveloped both girls in a hug.

My mom walked gently towards me with a sad smile and squeezed my hand as she leaned forward and kissed me. "I'm so proud of you right now," she whispered.

I'm snapped back to the present by the sound of a locker door being slammed shut and I can't help but wonder what Em would think of me right now.

Chapter 6

Ethan

I DIDN'T GO to school yesterday; the only reason I'm here today is to meet Blair for our study session. Dad lost his shit as soon as I got home Wednesday. He'd summoned me into the garage when I pulled up; I knew how it was going to play out as soon as I stepped out my car. I could see the look in his eyes. The man is permanently angry. I'd barely spoken three words before he delivered the first blow to my stomach; it immediately knocked all the air from me and dropped me to my knees. He must have had a particularly shitty day because he proceeded to deliver blow after blow until I'd finally passed out.

I should fight back, I've thought about it a million times. When I was younger I was scared shitless of him, afraid if I tried to fight back he would just come at me harder. I figured if I didn't retaliate, if I just stayed still and took it, that he would finish sooner. Like if he wasn't getting the fight that he wanted, he would quit. I've let him kick, punch and knock me around for so long now that I kind of feel like maybe I'm dead inside. Numb to the pain and shit he throws at me.

The older I get the more tired I am of walking on eggshells around him, tired of the beatings, just tired of my life. When he loses it and ends up in a blind rage, I shut down. I've prayed so many fucking times that this will be it, this will be the time he takes it too far. Throws one punch too many, kicks that little bit too hard, and just finishes me. At least then it would be over. My prayers go unanswered, though. Maybe it's because I have no faith in a higher being anymore. I know that Dad prays for forgiveness after he's calmed down. I've heard him a couple of times, maybe that's his idea of redemption. I have a hard time letting myself believe in a god that would forgive him; maybe I have it wrong though. All I know is that if there is a god, I must have done something pretty terrible in a past life to deserve this.

I couldn't have gone to school yesterday if I'd tried. I'm still sore as hell and it hurt just to breathe, there's no way I could've made it through practice without someone noticing that I couldn't even inhale properly without wincing. I need to be careful to not arouse suspicion. I've had too many near misses over the years with friends and even a teacher once asking how my home life was. I'm always on guard, making sure that I don't act like I'm in pain. Dad would not take well to questions being asked, and sitting straight-backed at a piano and playing for three hours just wasn't an option. He pushes and pushes for me to practice, to make sure that I get the scholarship to Eastman, and then beats me and puts me out of commission. I'm pretty sure the assholes bruised a rib again.

Mom found me in the garage, helped me into my room and came back with ice packs and taped me up. Her eyes were rimmed red from crying—same shit, different day. Didn't even look me in the eye. I fucking hate how weak she is. Why she's still with him, why she didn't protect me when I was younger, why she still doesn't protect me I'll never understand. That's a parent's job isn't it? To protect their kids. Dad must have missed that particular memo. Maybe if there had been a line dropped in when he took his law enforcement oath, "I promise to serve and protect, oh yeah, and not beat the living shit out of my son," things would be different.

Mom's more scared of him than I am and I get that, I really do, but I've pleaded with her to leave him. She won't do it, though, she's never gonna leave him. He has a hold over her; she's terrified of what he'd do if we did manage to escape and he found us. How can I blame her for that? The thought of it scares me too.

elle

"Yo, E! What's the plan for tonight?"

I take out my books from my locker and start loading them into my backpack.

"Am I driving or are you?" Jackson leans his shoulder on the locker next to mine as he takes a drink from his water bottle. We've just finished band practice and I'm in a world of pain right now. Having a guitar strapped across a bruised rib is no fun. I'm trying my damnedest not to let it show.

"I dunno man, I'm heading home to study with Blair. Maybe I'll just meet you guys there, not sure what time we'll get done."

"Ahhhh…Tutor Nerd's coming over, huh?"

I glare at him as I'm closing my locker. "Dude don't fucking call her that. Her name's Blair, she's cool."

"Whoa, who pissed on your cereal? You were calling her that just the other day," he says defensively, his palms held up by his chest.

"Do you like this girl? Wait, is that what the twenty questions were all about Wednesday?"

"Don't be a dick, Jackson, I was just trying to find out who she was. She's like a freaking enigma around here, she doesn't hang with anyone. I was curious is all."

My phone vibrates and I take it out of my pocket. "Shit, she's calling me now, just give me a minute."

"Hey, Blair," I answer in an all-too-eager voice. I start moving away from my locker and out of earshot from Jackson, who's eyeing me curiously.

"Hi, I was just checking to see if we were still on for tonight. The tutoring? You weren't in school yesterday. I didn't want to just turn up at your house if you were ill or something and I haven't seen you around today."

"Does that mean you've been looking for me? I'm flattered." I'm sure my smile is coming across in my voice.

"Easy there, are we still on or not?" she says, laughing.

I really like making this girl laugh.

"Yeah, we're still on, I'm just about to head home now. We should get there about the same time. If I'm not there before you I won't be long. My mom and dad won't be in, so just hang tight."

"Oh, okay. Guess I'll see you soon."

"Sure, bye," I say as I press end and turn back to where Jackson's standing with a big ass grin plastered across his smug face.

Jackson's my wingman; he's the all-American blonde blue-eyed boy next door. He's about six three, the same as me, but where he's built I'm leaner. The girls love him; they love us. At least they do until we've been in their pants and then forgotten their names. Doesn't stop them from coming back, though.

"What?" I say walking back over to him. He narrows his eyes at me shaking his head.

"Dude, don't lie to me, or yourself. I've known you forever—you like this girl, admit it."

"Fuck off, Jackson, I'll see you tonight" I call out, heading towards the exit.

"Have fun 'studying!'" he shouts, making air quotes with his fingers. I shake my head, suppressing a laugh, and carry on walking.

elle

I pull onto my drive and Blair looks over before carrying on playing ball. I always leave the basketball outside by the garage so I can go out and shoot hoops to clear my head. She lines up her shot and it rims the basket before falling through.

"Nice shot, Kobe Bryant."

She turns to look at me; her eyebrows are pinched together in confusion. It's pretty damn cute.

"Who?"

I groan, "Seriously, you've never heard of Kobe Bryant. Shit."

She laughs and picks her bag up from resting against the garage door. "Honestly, do I really look like a sports fan to you?"

I raise my eyebrows and take that as an invitation to check her out, her hair is piled up all messy on top of her head and she's wearing one of those t-shirts again, only this one's red. I suppress a laugh when I realize it says, 'Don't trust atoms. They make up everything.' My eyes continue their descent and stop at her legs, her sexy-as-sin legs. I'm sure I've just let out a groan. She's wearing a pair of denim cut-offs and some beat up black Chucks.

"No, you don't look like a sports fan, to be fair. I'd say you look like a librarian, but then the short shorts kind of threw me." I wink and stride towards the door to stop from staring at her legs any longer. I can already feel myself getting hard, and the last thing I need is my dick tenting the cargo shorts I'm wearing. It would be beyond awkward.

"A librarian? Really? Huh…I was going for geek chic, guess I missed my mark," she says, following me into the house.

I look back and she's smiling looking around at the pictures that line the hall. She seems to be oblivious to me watching her, lost in her own thoughts scanning each photo. It would be so nice to be that carefree in my own home, instead of constantly being on edge and worrying about what I'm gonna do next to set the asshole off.

"So your dad's a cop, huh?" she asks, eyeing the picture of him in his uniform, receiving some award a couple of years ago.

"Yeah, has been since I was born." My words are laced with disdain, I can't help it.

"You look really alike. Everyone always tells me that I look like my mom—she loves it when people ask if we're sisters. I'm pretty sure they're saying it just to be nice to her, but she eats that shit up. I never know whether to be pissed or not that they think I look like a forty-year-old."

I narrow my eyes and give her a once over. "Don't worry, you definitely don't look a day over thirty-five."

She tilts her chin at me. "Wow, you're just full of compliments today." She nudges my arm with her shoulder and then instantly takes a step away. I'm guessing it's not in her character to be as flirty as she's being. At least I hope this is flirting.

"Come on then, where are we studying?" she asks, looking down at her sneakers.

"Come on up to my room," I say and motion toward the stairs, "all my books are up there."

Her eyes widen slightly. "Won't your folks be pissed if they get home and you have some random girl in your room?"

A low laugh rumbles in my chest. "It wouldn't be the first time. Besides all we're doing is studying."

"I guess so," she says, making her way up the stairs and giving me a perfect view of her ass in those tiny shorts. "No need to worry about my parents, anyway. Mom won't be home until past eight and my dad's on night shift. We have the place to ourselves."

I move past her and open my bedroom door for her.

She walks straight over to my desk and starts unloading her bag.

"You wanna get your notes out and we can go through anything you didn't understand in class?"

"Sure," I say, but the only thing I don't understand at the moment is how I haven't noticed this girl until now.

ele

We've been in my room for a couple of hours and I'm getting ready to call it on the whole study session, I can't concentrate for shit. I keep watching Blair's legs as they swing back and forth from my desk chair. I'm fantasizing about how much I want them wrapped around me. I think I'm actually starting to get jealous of the stupid chair.

"How's about we leave it here for now? I think my head's gonna explode if I have to look at another equation." I close my book and rest back onto my elbows across my bed.

She peers up over the rim of her glasses. "Sure I'll head home in a sec. I'm guessing you want to get going to the party?" she says through a yawn.

"Why don't you come with me? We can chill, grab a drink, plus you'll get to watch us perform. You don't have other plans, do you?" Her eyes widen in shock and then I register that I've practically just asked her out on a date.

I don't think I've ever been so nervous about a girl's response before. In fact, scratch that, I have *never* been this worried. I've hooked up with tons of girls and never once given a shit about what they think of me. I'm not known for being the sweet and sensitive type. I'm more the asshole that sleeps with them and then doesn't call. Blair's different though; I don't want to be the cocky asshole around her. I don't just want to fuck her—which, by the way, I do—I want to spend time with her. I want her to like me, the real me. Not the self-assured musician front that I put on for everyone else..

Chapter 7

Blair

I HAVE DONE nothing for the last hour except pretend to read my textbook while stealing glances at Ethan. I've turned into the love-struck giddy teenager I used to laugh at Emily for being. I'm more than a little pissed at myself.

Ethan pulled up in his big ass black Camaro a couple minutes after I'd arrived. I was attempting to shoot hoops and had missed about fifty in a row and then fluked a shot just as he got out of his car. I wanted to do a happy dance!

He's wearing low-slung dark jeans and a tight grey beater. I can see the ridges of his abs and I think I would sell a kidney at this point to see them in the flesh. I have in the back of my mind that this guy's known for being a dick at school, but so far I haven't seen any trace of that Ethan. It's like he's turned into someone else. I can't figure him out.

I'm yawning and getting my things together when I hear him mumble something to me.

"Sorry, what?" He's looking kind of embarrassed and now I'm wondering what it could have been that I just missed.

"I asked if you wanted to come to TJ's party with me," he says, looking up at the ceiling instead of at me.

My first thought is to tell him no. Parties are definitely not my thing; they make me panic. I'm not overly comfortable with large groups of people, and being at one with him would make me feel even more awkward. What happens when he leaves me to go play with the band? I should just tell him what I told Casey and Brie. Em's letter flashes through my mind, stopping me from immediately turning his offer down. If I say yes, I could maybe cross a few things off that she wanted to do. Hell, if I went all out, I could go to the party with him, get wasted, do karaoke in front of everyone and then maybe even get him wasted enough to kiss me. That would pretty much nail half the list in one evening. I laugh out loud at the random stupidity of the thoughts running through my mind before realizing that Ethan asked me out, and all I've done in response is laugh. Shit.

"Okay, sure."

His eyes snap back to me and he's staring like I'm some weird creature he's never seen before. I'm immediately nervous and we haven't even left the room yet.

"For real?" He sounds surprised and it makes me smile.

"Yeah, Let me just text my mom and let her know I'll be late."

This was a stupid ass idea. We've been here all of thirty seconds and I'm ready to leave. I walked through the door with Ethan and it was as if someone had killed the music: all eyes were on us instantly. It feels like every female here is shooting me daggers. I've always flown under the radar at school, but apparently walking into a party with Ethan Jamison garners some attention. I thought maybe it would earn me cool points but looking at the stares I'm receiving, I'm pretty sure I've just topped every girl's bitch list.

Ethan shifts his guitar case into the opposite hand and takes a hold of mine, lacing our fingers together. I feel a jolt of electricity race up my arm, awakening every nerve in my body. I can't believe he's holding my hand. I'm silently praying that they're not going to go all clammy and gross, I don't want him to know how much of an affect he's having on me, it would be beyond embarrassing.

"Let's go grab a drink and find the guys," he states, weaving us in and out of the crowded hall and into the kitchen that's filled with even more of my fellow students. Looking around, I'm pretty sure I've never spoken to any of them. Someone pushes back into us as we enter and I stumble a little into Ethan's side.

"Yikes, sorry," I tell him, noticing a look of pain flash across his face. I'm not exactly heavy and didn't think I'd knocked into him that hard, but from that wince, you'd think a linebacker just tackled him.

"Blairrrrrr!"

I whip my head round to see Casey barging through the crowded room heading straight for me, with an open-mouthed Brie hot on her heels.

"Oh my god, you made it! And with arm candy, too! I'm impressed," Case says as she envelops me in hug. I stand awkwardly with my hand still clasped in Ethan's.

"Sup Casey, Brie…you guys seen Jackson anywhere?" Ethan asks as I stand like a mute. The fact that he knows them both by name shouldn't bother me but it kind of does.

"He's out by the pool with TJ and a few others," Brie replies. Her eyes are trained on me and a bewildered smile is slowly growing across her face.

"Okay, I'm just gonna go say hi. I'll grab us some drinks and be right back." Ethan drops my hand and disappears into the crowd.

"You got three-seconds to spill it, girl!"

Before I can even register what Casey means, Brie is bombarding me with questions left right and center.

"Oh my god, oh my god, oh my god! What are you doing here with Ethan Jamison? Why did you not let us know you were coming? Wait, were you two just holding hands? Oh god, are you on a date? You are, aren't you? You're on a date with Ethan Jamison." Brie fires at me, hardly stopping to take a breath. She's bouncing about completely animated and her boobs are in danger of making an appearance from the handkerchief-sized shirt she has them squeezed into. The guy behind her is completely ignoring what the girl he's with is saying; his eyes are glued to Brie, waiting for the show.

"We are not on a date…well, not really. We were studying, he was headed here and asked if I wanted to come is all," I tell her, grabbing her arm and repositioning her to block the creeper's view.

"Right, so you'll come if Ethan asks you but not us?"

Brie says wiggling her eyebrows at me.

"Still doesn't answer why you guys were holding hands," Case interjects in a singsong voice.

"Jeez, guys! He was just leading me through here," I say, trying not to smile and give away the fact that I was really enjoying the whole handholding thing.

"Mm-hmm," she replies with an exaggerated side-to-side head movement, her eyebrows raised in a 'what ever you say' expression.

"My god, that boy's hot!" Brie chimes back in. "Seriously, like what's your deal? I've been trying to get his attention for months. The guy will practically sleep with anything that walks except me!"

Case and I look at one another for a beat before bursting out in a fit of laughter. Suddenly Brie's eyes grow large as Ethan steps beside us, passing me a red solo cup filled with a sickly pink-looking liquid. He notices me examining the contents of the cup.

"Relax, it's just punch, or at least that's what TJ said it was. Half the cheer squad is drinking it, so it can't be that bad."

"Uh-huh. So, why is it you grabbed yourself a beer?" I tilt my chin motioning to the bottle he's holding.

"What? I'm not drinking a chick drink," he says, smiling. "I have a reputation to uphold."

ele

I'm officially wasted! It's kind of lame that I'm eighteen years old and have never been drunk, but Em was diagnosed with leukemia when we were fifteen. She started on treatment straight away, so partying and getting trashed were pretty low down on her list of priorities. There was no way in hell I was going to go do that myself when my best friend couldn't. So yeah, this is my first real party and the first time I've ever drunk enough to feel like everything is going in slow motion, but it's cool. Everyone is super funny. I like the floaty feeling that seems to have overtaken me.

Kickstart played an hour set out on the patio and I was completely mesmerized. Ethan had told me that they were about to play and asked if I would watch, and given that I haven't been able to move my gaze from him for more than two minutes all night, it was an easy question to answer.

Jackson is their drummer; Drew plays bass and Ethan the guitar. Both Drew and Ethan sing. To say watching him perform was hot would be a complete understatement. He's so self-assured it borders on arrogant but completely works in his favor. They played a few original songs but mainly covers. A semi-circle of girls formed, surrounding them as they played Coldplay's *Magic*. I couldn't tear my attention away from him with his eyes shut so tightly singing the lyrics into the mic. I'm pretty sure every female here sighed at how completely beautiful and totally hot it was. As soon as the set was finished Ethan made his way over to me and led me back into the kitchen where some guys were playing drinking games.

Apparently, according to Jackson and Brie, my hand-eye coordination sucks, which is why I'm bad at beer pong, and subsequently why I'm so drunk.

I am leaning against Ethan and he keeps trying to get me to drink more water. I've told him that I was happy drinking the punch. He confiscated that and it's probably good because it feels as though my lips are stuck to my teeth. Suddenly *Hey Mickey* is blasting from the speakers and Casey claps her hands excitedly.

"I freaking love this song! It was in that film, um…what's it called? Ugh, you know the one I mean, right? The one with Fat Amy."

I giggle snort. "Ooooh, the one with the cup song!" I offer and am graced with blank stares from the crowd of people that have gathered around us.

"Oh my god, you must know which one I mean."

"I do!" Case exclaims. "My little sister has been trying to learn it for the last month."

I laugh and proceed to tell the group that I, in fact, am awesome at the cup song. Ethan nudges my shoulder and leans down to whisper low enough for only me to hear, "Don't just bring it, sing it."

I whirl my head around to look at him; it's too fast and I almost lose my balance. "You do know it!"

"Sure I do, the main girl was hot," he says, winking at me. I've decided it must be his thing. Winking.

"Come on then, Blair!" Jackson announces. "Show us."

It's a challenge and I'm feeling nervous all of a sudden. I take a deep breath and square my shoulders. The alcohol must have done something to my sense of fear because I stride over to the kitchen counter and pick up a solo cup. The room falls quiet as someone kills the music. Great.

I take a deep breath and look up to see Ethan's face smiling at me. It's all the encouragement I need so I begin performing the song to a room full of drunken gawking teenagers.

Chapter 8

Ethan

BLAIR IS BEYOND wasted; she completely floored everyone with her cup song. The whole place was silent as she weaved some sort of magic spell on us with her raspy voice. It was beautiful. She's beautiful. She went to get a drink and disappeared for way longer than I was comfortable with. I started looking for her and found her out back doing shots with TJ, Corey, Drew and Liam, another guy from the volleyball team. Dannii and a few of the cheer squad were chanting for her to down them.

"The fuck, guys?" I roar, barging through the little circle that surrounds her. "You can see she's had way too much, why are you letting her drink more?"

"Lighten up man, she's a big girl, she can take care of herself," Corey offers as he stands practically undressing her with his eyes.

I don't even have time to think before I push Corey out of my way and grab Blair's hand, dragging her back through the house and away from the set of dicks trying to get her completely messed up.

"Wait, slow down, you're hurting my arm," she says, stumbling behind me.

"Shit, I'm sorry." I drop her hand immediately and turn to meet her eyes.

"I didn't mean to hurt you, honestly." I roll my shoulders. "I think it's time we leave."

People are watching with way too much interest as I place my hand at the small of her back and walk us through the crowded hall and out of the front door.

"I'm sorry if I've embarrassed you," she says once we get outside.

"Wait what? No, of course you haven't embarrassed me, I just want to get you home, make sure you're gonna be okay." I suck in a deep breath and blow it out slowly.

"Trust me, you're gonna feel like hell in the morning after what you've put away." I take her hand again and lead her to my car. I pull open the door for her and she stops dead in her tracks, narrowing her eyes.

"You've been drinking, I'm not getting in there with you." I smile wide. Even drunk she's smart.

"I only had two beers; I'm good," I assure her before sitting her in the passenger seat and buckling it.

I barely pull out of the drive before she's asleep with her head resting against the window. I try waking her to ask where she lives, but all I get is a string of incoherent mumbles. I contemplate going through her purse to find her cell and call her mom, but I don't know if that's such a good idea given the state she's in. I war with myself about taking her back to my house before I decide to let her sleep off the alcohol in the pool house. Dad won't be home until mid-morning and he almost never goes out back. It'll be fine, plus her car is still at my place since I drove us to TJ's.

I've laid Blair on the futon in the pool house after carrying her from my car. She weighs next to nothing but my ribs still hurt and it's left me out of breath. I pull her Chucks off and place a blanket over her.

"Ethan?" Her sleep-strained voice breaks through the silence.

"Yeah, I'm here."

"I don't feel so good."

Shit. I pull back the blanket and scoop her up into my arms walking as fast as I can towards the bathroom. My chest is burning with pain and I'm trembling as I go to place her on the floor but I'm too late. The contents of her stomach explode all over my t-shirt, and I have to hold my breath so I don't start to gag and puke too. I position her over the toilet while she continues to heave out the gallons of punch she must have consumed.

She's shaking like mad as I push back the hair from her face and rub small circles on her back. The tears start to stream under her glasses and down her flushed cheeks.

"I'm so sorry," she cries.

"Shush, it's fine," I tell her in a hushed tone. "You think you're about done?"

"I don't know," she hiccups. "My head won't stop spinning, I'm scared to move." She drops her head back down onto her arms currently holding the toilet in a tight embrace.

"I'm never drinking again. Why would people do this voluntarily?"

I smile and resist the urge to tell her that she should have listened to me and switched to water hours ago.

"Don't worry, you'll start to feel better soon." I look down at my t-shirt and instantly wish I hadn't. I need to change before I start gagging. I stand and peel the shirt off, dropping it outside the shower. Blair looks up at me, then quickly removes her glasses and wipes them on the hem of her t-shirt before replacing them. Her eyes widen and she gasps. I follow her gaze to my chest and then freeze. Fuck. The bruises are pretty evident. They're all over my ribs in varying shades of purple and yellow. Why the hell did I take my shirt off in front of her? I know better than that. Hell, I've had enough practice.

"What—" she hiccups, "what happened to you?"

Her voice is laced with concern, intrigue and sadness. I hate it.

"It's nothing, don't worry about it." *Please don't question it, I don't want to lie.*

"It looks like a pretty big something to me, who did it? Have you told your parents? Your dad?"

My body instantly tenses at her mentioning the asshole and she notices before I can try to relax my shoulders.

"Blair, it's nothing just leave it…please." It's a plea and I drop my head between my shoulders and sigh. Her body is still wrapped around the toilet but I can feel her gaze burning into me, searing into my soul.

"Ethan, does this have something to do with your dad? Every time I bring him up you flinch."

Her next words come out as a whisper.

"Did he do this?"

I don't look up as I reply. "Listen, it's not as bad as you think. Let's just get you cleaned up. I'll explain. I will. Just not now."

"Promise?"

I let out a defeated breath. "Okay."

I attempt the help her up before she grabs a hold of the toilet again.

"Oh god, don't move me."

An amused chuckle escapes my chest. "Okay, Princess, sit tight and I'll be right back."

I go and grab the blanket from the futon and walk back into the bathroom. She looks like she's passed out again. I drop to the floor beside her and position her back to my chest. I wrap the blanket over my shoulders and envelope us both in its warmth. She mumbles something incoherent about crossing off her list. I'm not sure; she isn't making a whole lot of sense. She presses her head back under my chin and I listen as her breath falls into the steady slow rhythm of sleep. She's going to want answers when she wakes up. I don't know if I can give them to her. But for the first time in my life, I want to. I want to tell this girl everything. I want this girl, period.

Chapter 9

Blair

I'M DYING. THERE'S no other explanation for how I'm feeling right now. My head is going to explode, my eyes don't want to open, and I'm too hot. Way too hot. I attempt to stretch and my body is held in place. My eyes snap open, sending a blinding shot of pain straight across my forehead. I squeeze them shut for a second and then I open them again and try to focus.

There's a large set of arms folded in my lap that aren't mine. What the hell? I turn and see I'm encased in Ethan's arms. His head is tipped back and he's snoring ever so lightly. I'm jammed between his body and the toilet and I need to get up and get some air. Nothing makes sense. I try to move again and my stomach rolls. I feel like I'm going to be sick. Then it hits me. Why I'm sleeping next to a toilet. The party. The drinking. The bruises. Now I really do think I'm going to be sick.

Ethan stirs and I take the opportunity to slip out of his

embrace and crawl across the floor using the basin as an anchor as I pull myself up. I'm greeted with my reflection in the vanity mirror, and I wince at the sight that stares back at me. The little mascara I was wearing is now smudged under my eyes, my pale skin has a grey hue to it, and it looks as though birds could nest in my hair. My mouth feels like I've been chewing on sand and I look around to see if I can find any toothpaste. There's a bottle of mouthwash next to the basin; I take a sip, swilling it around and around to kill the taste of stale alcohol and vomit. I pull my hair free of its tie and try to smooth it out with my fingers.

"Morning, sunshine."

I freeze in place, not wanting to turn around and have him see the state I'm in.

"God Ethan, I don't even know where to begin…I'm so sorry that yo—"

"There's no need to apologize, Blair, we've all been there."

I can hear the smile in his voice and instinctively I turn towards it. He's standing now. Shirtless. My eyes travel from his broad shoulders down to the bruises that mar his otherwise flawless skin. The deep ridges of his abs are within touching distance and I can't drag my eyes away from them. My mouth suddenly feels like a desert again and I have no clue what to say to him.

I feel awkward; full of shame that I let myself get so drunk that he had to take care of me, and full of sadness that anyone would hurt this guy. This funny, cute, amazing guy. And what's worse, I'm pretty sure he's gonna confirm that the one doing the hurting is the one person on this planet who's supposed to protect him.

"I should have listened to you and switched to drink-ing water when you said. I can't believe you've seen me puking." I shake my head in disbelief at this whole situa-tion. "I'll be out of your hair in a few minutes. I need to get home, my mom's gonna freak that I didn't come home last night."

"Yeah, about that…I'm sorry. You kinda passed out in my car and I didn't know your address. I tried waking you but you were pretty wasted." His arms are crossed behind his neck and he's eyeing me as if he's unsure of himself.

"Are you seriously apologizing to me right now? I can't bel—" I'm cut short by the sound of the pool house door swinging open and an angry booming male voice shouting Ethan's name. It must be his dad. I watch as Ethan's eyes widen in panic, and I'm pretty sure mine look the same.

"Wait here, okay? I'll be back in a minute." Before I can even breathe a response, he's out of the bathroom, leaving me alone, not knowing what to do. I want to get out of here as quickly as I can. I scan the room but there's no sign of my purse and I'm too scared to leave this room to go looking for it. Why did he sound so angry? I'm al-most positive it will have to do with me and if so, I can't just stand here and let him take the blame. Especially if I'm right about where his bruises came from.

I creep over to the door and open it as quietly as I can. I can hear a heated conversation in hushed tones. I'm guessing that's for my benefit. I straighten my shoulders, take a deep breath and head in the direction of the voices. Every instinct I have is screaming for me to turn around and go back into the bathroom like Ethan asked.

It feels like the air in this building has been sucked out and replaced by palpable tension. My heart is pounding against my chest and my hung-over head feels dizzy. Every step I take towards them ramps up my anxiety by tenfold. My whole body is shaking and I'm not sure if it's because of the alcohol that's still in my system, or from the adrenaline surging through my veins. I turn the corner and enter the room where Ethan and his father are standing.

They're standing nose to nose in a standoff, and although Ethan's eyes are downcast, I can see his fists balled tightly by his sides. The muscles in his arms are flexing with the tension. His dad's face is pulled into a sneer and I'm struggling to understand what it is that Ethan did to warrant the look of pure hatred in his dad's eyes. I take another step and his face instantly smoothes when he notices me enter the room. Ethan's head turns slowly towards me as he tracks his dad's gaze and there's such an intense sadness in his eyes that my heart literally aches.

"Make sure she gets home and I want you straight back here, you understand?" His dad says forcing a smile in my direction and then he turns and heads out the door. Before I register I'm even moving I've closed the distance between us and stop just a foot away.

"Are you okay?" I ask, my voice barely above a whisper. Our eyes are locked on each other and I want so desperately to take the extra step and wrap my arms around him tightly. Tell him that the hatred I just witnessed in his dad's eyes isn't normal, and that there must be something seriously fucked with him. That's not how a father should act towards his son.

"He's stressed with work, there's talk of him being made to take early retirement," he offers with a weak smile and my stomach rolls. He's making excuses for him. I feel like I'm going to be sick.

"Are your bruises from him?" I choke out. I know it's direct but I want to know the truth. There's a long silence, minutes feel like hours and neither one of us break our stare. The air between us is charged with so much emotion I feel like I'll combust if he doesn't say something soon. My heart is pleading for him to say no, there's a perfectly good explanation, and it's all just a misunderstanding. But my head is in disagreement. "Ethan?" I whisper.

"Yes."

My stomach plummets and I have an overwhelming urge to cry. I swallow the knot in my throat and will my voice not to crack.

"Does he do it a lot?"

"Depends on what your idea of a lot is. It's not every day, sometimes it's not even every week, but it's pretty regular."

"Shit, Ethan that's not right. Have you told your mom? Does she know this is happening?" I want to comfort him, make him feel better, hell, make myself feel better, but I have absolutely no idea what to do or say to take away the pain I can see in his eyes.

"She knows."

His voice sounds completely dejected and I can't take it. I close the gap between us and throw my arms around him, hugging him as hard as I dare. He stands frozen for a second before I feel his arms snake around my back and pull me into his chest tighter. He rests his chin in the crook of my neck and I suddenly get the feeling that he hasn't been hugged in a long time.

Chapter 10

Ethan

SHE WALKED IN on us. I told her to stay in the bathroom; I didn't want her to meet the asshole. He was in the middle of telling me what a worthless piece of shit I am, and he wanted to know whose car was blocking the drive. I don't know if she heard any of the conversation. I hope she didn't. I told him it belonged to some girl from school. I don't want him to know anything about her. I try to keep my worlds separate. The Ethan Jamison that attends West Point High who's loud, outgoing, and probably a little arrogant is a completely different guy from Ethan Jamison, son of Frank and Moira Jamison, eternal screw-up and all around disappointment. Sometimes I feel like a fucking schizophrenic. It's tiring as hell, but with Blair it's different. I feel like I don't need to put on the act. It's as if she has no expectations of me—it's liberating, really. If she doesn't expect anything then I sure as hell can't let her down.

Her arms tighten around me and break me from my thoughts. I want to stay wrapped up in her forever; she's warm and soft and fits perfectly against me. I know the second we move apart she's going to want more answers, and truthfully, I want to give her them, but I'm scared she'll see me as some weak pathetic wreck. I'm not cool with that, I hate feeling weak. I spend my whole goddamn life trying to act anything but. The last thing on this planet I want is her pity. I don't think I could take it.

"God, Ethan I'm so sorry." She steps back to look at me and her eyes are glazed over like she's about to cry. Fuck, I hope she doesn't cry, not over me. "Do they hurt still?" She motions to my bruised ribs.

"They're not too bad, I can deal," I answer, trying to make my voice sound lighter.

"You shouldn't have to deal! What's happening isn't right. You need to tell someone. He can—"

I cut her off before she can finish her sentence.

"Tell who? Huh, my mom knows and does shit about it, I can't tell the police. For fuck's sake Blair, he *is* the goddamn police! Who am I supposed to tell?"

She lets out a sob but it doesn't deter me and I carry on. "I'm eighteen, a legal adult, and as soon as I graduate I'm outta here. I just need to suck it up for a few more months until college."

"But…but," she hiccups and her eyes are pleading with me to tell someone.

"Blair, I can't tell anyone and neither can you. Okay? Do you understand me? I don't want to tell anyone, and I don't want you to tell anyone either. You have to promise me. It'll be over soon. Promise you won't say anything.

Please."

She takes a step forward and takes both my hands, linking our fingers.

"I promise," she says in a whisper that's almost inaudible. She's looking down at her feet and I need to see her face.

"Blair, look at me."

She lifts her head slowly and her cheeks are blotchy and wet from the tears she couldn't hold back.

"Hey, don't cry," I say, trying to soothe her. "I'm okay, everything will be okay. Honestly."

"Okay...look, what if I talk to my mom, see if you can stay with us? I don't need to tell her the truth, she's cool she—"

Her sad voice feels like a knife to my skin, it hurts worse than a blow to the gut and I interrupt her. "I can't leave my mom. Not like that, he'd go fucking nuts. He's all for me going to college, if I up and left now, I don't know what he'd do. I just need to wait a few more months."

We stand in silence for what feels like forever, the air around us thick with sadness, anger and frustration. Something has changed between us. It feels tangible. There's a comfort level, a trust that I've never experienced with anyone. Ever. I'm hit with the realization that this girl may just have the power to hurt me more than that asshole ever could. The knowledge leaves me feeling raw and exposed. Blair Thomas could destroy me, but somehow I know she won't.

I collect Blair's purse out of my car and let her freshen up while I run to the laundry and grab a clean shirt. When I return to the pool house she's sitting on the futon talking to her mom on the phone. I can hear her mom's high-pitched angry voice from all the way across the room. Blair's nose is wrinkled and she's holding the cell away from her ear as her mom spouts off something about being irresponsible. I offer her a weak smile; I feel bad that she's in trouble. I should have looked through her cell and texted her mom last night to let her know she was safe. I'm an idiot.

She finishes the call and throws her cell into her purse on the floor, falling back into the seat with a groan.

"Well, that went down well," she sighs.

"How bad was it? She sounded pretty pissed. I could hear her from all the way over here."

"Let's just say I'm probably grounded until I'm thirty; that was the first—and more than likely the last—party I'll ever go to."

A laugh escapes me and I can't help but grin. "Good job. You made the most of it then, huh? I'm pretty sure you'll be a legend at school on Monday. You out drunk most the guys on the volleyball team."

"Oh, god," she groans, pulling her glasses off and pinching the bridge of her nose between her thumb and finger. "I can't believe I sang in front of all of them. I'll be a complete laughing stock."

"Are you kidding me right now? You were amazing. Trust me, no one will be laughing at you. In fact you kind of stole the band's thunder."

Her cheeks redden at the compliment and I think it's

my new favorite thing about her. I can make her blush.

"So, anyway…you gonna tell me what this list is you were mumbling on about last night in the bathroom?"

Her head snaps up and her eyes lock on me. They look so much greener without her glasses. She looks totally different. Kinda like when Clark Kent takes his glasses off and suddenly he's no longer a geek. It's like I knew she was hot before but fuck me, now she's beautiful.

"I told you about the list?"

"No, not really, you just kept mumbling something about having to cross off the list." My interest is suddenly magnified a billion percent at the panicked look on her face right now.

"So, you gonna tell me what it is?"

"It's personal, I'd rather not. It's kind of…um, it's just…"

Truthfully, I'm a little hurt that after what's just unfolded between us, she can't tell me about a stupid list. The hurt must be evident on my face. She replaces her glasses and looks back at me.

"Look, okay. Emily, my best friend, died a few months back and she'd written me this letter with a list attached, kind of like a bucket list. She'd written down things that she wanted to do before she died. There were still things that she hadn't crossed off. She wants me to finish it for her. I haven't told anyone about it, I don't think she would have wanted me to. I know it sounds crazy but it's the last thing she's ever asked of me, so I feel like I need to do it for her."

"It doesn't sound crazy at all." I say crossing the room and sitting beside her.

"Yeah well, one of the items on her list was to get

wasted."

"Wait, so you're telling me that she'd never been drunk?" I say, disbelief clear in my voice.

"Neither of us had." She shrugs her shoulders and carries on.

"She was diagnosed with Acute Lymphoblastic Leukemia when we were fifteen. She started chemotherapy the day after she found out. She was on so many drugs to try control the cancer, she couldn't have gotten drunk even if she'd wanted to—it would have screwed with her treatment. She was my best friend; we did everything together. I wasn't about to leave her at home and start partying without her… I mean what kind of friend would do that, right? Obviously, it must have bothered her more than I realized because she put it on her bucket list."

Wow, now I feel like a complete dick for not believing she'd never been drunk.

"So, at least you got to tick off one of her things then, huh?" I say. "I'm pretty sure she'd have been impressed with your efforts."

"Yeah well, I actually managed to cross off two with the whole singing in front of half the senior class."

She's smiling but shaking her head at the same time, like she can't believe what she did.

"Em wanted to be a singer, she had an amazing voice, too. I can hold a note, but seriously she was like Adele or something, her voice was that good. Thing is, she was super confident about everything except singing in front of people—she just couldn't do it. Too nervous, I suppose. Performing to a crowed was on her list too. Do you think last night classifies as a crowd?"

"Definitely," I offer, "and you nailed that too."

She blushes again and it takes every ounce of strength in me not to lean over and kiss her. I want to pin her down and completely posses her. Kiss every part of her. Taste every part of her. Bite down on that plump bottom lip, and run my hands over her soft creamy skin. But I can't let myself go there, not yet. When I do finally kiss her, and I definitely will, I want her to remember it forever, without it being tainted by the memory of how this morning started out.

I can't resist her, though, so I give in a little to the temptation and lean forward, placing a feather-light kiss to her forehead. I think I must have shocked the hell out of her because she's sitting like a statue not moving, I can't even hear her breathe. I'm officially starting to panic when she seems to shake off whatever the hell that was and smiles. I relax and smile back.

"Come on, Princess, I think it's time I get you home."

Chapter 11

Blair

I'VE MADE A promise that I don't think I can keep. He asked me not to tell anyone about his situation and I agreed I wouldn't. I regret it already. I have to tell someone. It's not right what's happening to him. I snatch the keys from my purse and follow him out of the pool house to my car.

"Keys." He holds his hand out expectantly.

"Huh?"

"Keys," he repeats. "You can't drive after the amount you drank last night. You'll probably still be over the limit."

"Oh, right… yeah, okay," I say, tossing my keys to him. I throw like a girl and he has to lunge forward to catch them.

"I'll drive you home and walk back."

"You can't do that," I say, feeling guilty that I probably wrecked his night and now I'm dominating his morning, too.

"Sure I can, plus it means I get to spend more time with you."

His crooked smile causes his dimples to flash and it just about melts me on the spot. I smile and climb into the passenger side of my car. He gets in and I immediately burst out laughing. He's in the driver's seat folded like a pretzel with his knees up near his chin.

"Jeez, how short *are* you?" he says, laughing while adjusting the seat so he's not sandwiched against the steering wheel.

"Hey now, God grows things until they're perfect," I say, grinning back at him. "I guess some of us take less time than others."

"That's so cheesy," he laughs. "Tell me that's not a line from one of your t-shirts."

I stay quiet and his head whips around from adjusting the mirrors.

"It is, isn't it? You have a t-shirt that says that."

"Some people quote Plato, I prefer quoting my shirts." I shrug and he laughs again and I smile at how much I like the sound.

We spend almost the entire car ride in a comfortable silence. It's as if something between us has shifted, a barrier that I wasn't even aware of until its disappearance, removed. He's confided in me about his father, trusted me with something I'm pretty sure even his best friends don't know about. We hardly know one and other and yet I feel weirdly close to him. He trusts me to keep my promise and I'm not entirely sure how I feel about that. I give him directions to my house and he pulls onto the drive and turns off the engine, shifting in his seat to look at me.

"So…I'll see you at school, I guess?"

"Yep," I respond letting the p pop.

"Look Blair, I know you've already promised me bu—"

I hold my hand up to stop him. "I won't say anything, but I can't pretend that I think it's the right thing."

"Thank you."

"I better go in and face the inquisition," I say, motioning to the house.

"Yeah, I should go too," he says, although he makes no attempts to get out of the car. We sit holding each other's gaze for a few moments before he leans forward and presses a light kiss to my forehead. "Later, Princess," he says and then just like that, he's gone. I'm left sitting in the passenger seat with a goofy grin on my face but a heavy sadness in my heart.

elle

To say that my mom was pissed with me for not coming home is a major understatement. I can't remember a time that she's been this mad. She told me that I was technically an adult so she wasn't about to ground me, but she expects me to start acting like one. Staying out all night and getting drunk was unacceptable and she was disappointed in me. Pot. Kettle. Black!

To be fair, I was disappointed in myself too. If Ethan hadn't taken me home when he did, who knows what would have happened. I spent the rest of Saturday in bed feeling hung over to hell. I woke this morning from a dreamless sleep and decided that I needed to talk to someone about Ethan, so here I am. About to break my promise.

ele

"Hey Emily," I say, sitting Indian-style beside her grave. I lay down the yellow sunflowers I brought with me and speak quietly as if she were right here with me, which I guess she sort of is.

"I decided to make a start on your list. I think you'd be pretty impressed with me. So far I've managed to get wasted—totally overrated, by the way—and the hangover was hell. Add in the fact that I puked on Ethan Jamison while he was taking care of me, and I think it's safe to say I won't be drinking again anytime soon. Trust me, you aren't missing much. Also, I sang to a crowd. Well, technically it was to half the senior class and volleyball team at TJ Connor's party. I'm kinda dreading showing up to school tomorrow."

I pull a few blades of grass out the ground and twist them together before continuing. I tell her about tutoring Ethan, the party and the abuse. I tell her everything, holding nothing back.

"Em I don't know what to do. I should tell someone, right? But he made me promise and what if I tell someone and nothing happens to his dad and I just make it worse? God, I hate feeling like this, I wish I didn't know...that's a bitch thing to say isn't it? I'm horrid. I just really like him, Em. I feel guilty as hell for liking him because it's Ethan. *Your* Ethan. Are you mad at me? I'm mad at me! This is like breaking Girl Code 101. I promise I didn't mean to like him; when he turned up at the study session the other day I was expecting him to be a douche and he isn't. He's awkward and funny and kind and sorta beautiful. I don't want to like him, Emily, honestly I don't, but I can't help it. Shit, I wish you were here."

My vision is suddenly blurry; I didn't realize I was crying. I take my glasses off and wipe at my eyes with the sleeve of my sweater. It's a pointless task though, and the more I try to wipe away the tears, the more they fall.

"Tell me what to do, Em." I sit for a long time just staring at the rolled-up blades of grass in my hand, waiting for an answer I know isn't coming. The sky's turning gray and a cold breeze is blowing through the trees. I pull my sweater tighter around me and say goodbye. I don't know what I was expecting coming to speak to Emily. Maybe just to try and make sense of the situation and to feel better by telling someone about Ethan. Or, maybe to shed the guilt of feeling like I may be falling for him...I'm not sure. I just know that it didn't work: I still feel guilty, I still feel afraid, and I still don't know what the hell I'm supposed to do.

Chapter 12

Ethan

I SPENT ALL day Saturday thinking about her, I spent all day Sunday thinking about her, and now I'm early to school to see if I can catch her before classes start. It's official. I'm whipped. I've turned into Drew. I walk to my locker on autopilot, paying zero attention to my surroundings, too busy thinking about Blair.

"Hey Rock Star, what happened to you Saturday night?"

Shit! Della matches my stride and is staring at me expectantly. She's wearing her cheer uniform; it's so small it looks like it's been shrunk in the wash. Don't get me wrong, I'm not complaining. She has a smoking hot body. I make a mental note not to stare at her tits and try to maintain eye contact.

"Sup, Del?"

"I turned up late to TJ's and you were MIA. Jackson said you'd left with some girl. Am I being replaced?"

She's twisting her long red hair around her finger and pouting at me. Della's cool, she knows the score—we're friends with benefits, just without the friends bit. She steers me into a classroom and leans her hip against one of the desks.

"Yeah, about that. I don't think our arrangement's gonna work for me anymore." I know it's straight to the point, but I don't want there to be any misunderstanding. She moves forward and places her hand against my chest, leaning close so she can whisper in my ear.

"Let me know when you're bored of this one. I'll be waiting."

I narrow my eyes in confusion. What's that supposed to mean? Her words register and I pull back. Instantly I know Blair is behind me, I can feel her presence.

Della steps forward again kissing me on the cheek. "See you around, E." She disappears and takes her seat.

I spin around to Blair and I feel like a dick. She's eying me like I'm a dick too. Not good!

"Della 'I'm gonna fuck your fella' Fields...really?" Her nose is scrunched up in disgust and I can't help the laugh that escapes.

"Della what? Is that what people call her?"

"Is that a serious question?"

"She's not that bad," I say, trying to keep a straight face. If I didn't know any better I'd swear Blair looked jealous.

"Look, I'm not saying she's promiscuous, I'm just surprised that Facebook hasn't made her panties a place to check in, yet!"

I instantly throw my head back and laugh so hard my

eyes water. "Shit, you don't hold back do you?"

Her cheeks redden slightly and she bites her bottom lip. Fuck, I want to do that for her.

"Sorry, that was kind of harsh, huh? I shouldn't judge. She's just got one helluva reputation!"

I'm aware that she's talking to me but I'm too busy letting my eyes roam all over her body to listen. She's in skinny jeans that are so tight they look like they've been sprayed on and she's wearing sneakers and a plaid shirt. Then it hits me.

"Hey, no slogan tee today?"

"Nope, not today." She's sporting a huge grin.

I'm about to reply when Jackson, Drew and TJ appear behind Blair, batting their eyelashes and acting all dreamy. Drew decides to start pretending to rub his nipples behind her like a complete dick while grinning at me. The other two are trying not to bust out laughing like idiots. Blair notices me trying to kill them with my stare and turns to see what's caught my attention.

"This isn't your class, why are you all in here?"

"We noticed E and came to drag him away from the party animal herself! Recovered yet?" TJ asks, putting an arm around her shoulders like they've been friends for years. I instantly want to rip it off and beat him with it for touching her. I'm not a territorial person normally, and I've been friends with TJ for years, but hell if seeing his hands on her doesn't make me want to piss in a circle around her, beat my goddamn chest and shout 'mine'.

"Yo, guys, give us a second, will you?" I pull Blair out from under TJ's arm and maneuver her out into the hall.

"Wanna meet me at lunch today?" I ask, trying to

school my voice so that I don't sound like some desperate pussy.

"Actually, I can't today. I was cornered by Casey and Brie the second I got out of my car. I actually came over to see if everything was okay when you got back from taking me home Saturday."

Her words are like a bucket of ice water over my head. Completely killing my good mood.

"I'm guessing that you mean with my dad? Yeah, um everything was fine…he was in bed by the time I got home. He'd been on night shift." I clear my throat and try to hide the disappointment of her rejection in my voice. "Look, you don't need to worry or feel sorry for me or shit like that. I don—"

"I can't pretend not to be concerned about you, Ethan. I don't pity you if that's what you're thinking. I just wanted to make sure you were okay," she says, eyeing the floor. "I care."

Her words slide over me like a warm blanket. *I care*. I know about the list from her friend and she knows about my dad; we've shared secrets and yet never shared a kiss. I need to remedy that. I feel like I'll die right here and now if I don't. I take a step closer to her and lift her chin with my finger so she's looking up at me. The atmosphere around us is cracking with electricity and our surroundings fade as I watch her eyes widen, realizing my intention.

She inhales a sharp breath; I angle my face and move slowly closer to hers, my gaze zeroing in on her lips. I can feel her breath fan across me and there are barely millimeters between our mouths. Adrenaline is pumping through my veins and my whole body feels like it's on fire. My hearts slamming against my chest as her eyes drift shut. I'm about to press my lips against hers, finally taste her kisses...then the bell sounds for first period and her eyes snap open. She moves back and my hand drops from her face. She looks startled and a little disappointed. Just like that, the moments lost. I want to fucking scream at how badly I want to kiss this girl. Instead I take a step back, flash her my best 'I'm a fucking boss' smile and tell her, "To be continued Princess," before winking and then turning away, walking as fast as I can to class while holding my jacket in front of me to hide my goddamn semi.

Chapter 13

Blair

"GIRL, YOU'D BETTER spill it before Brie has a breakdown!" Casey says, linking her left arm with mine. I don't have a chance to even think of responding before Brie has ambushed me on my right side and linked arms too. I'm being escorted to the cafeteria for interrogation and I'm starting to panic.

"Before anything else, you need to tell me if you're dating Ethan Jamison," Brie says, marching me through the halls as fast as she can.

"Um, no. Why would you think I'm dating him?"

Both girls come to an abrupt stop and I'm jerked backwards as though on a giant bungee.

"Kellie told Tammy, who saw Lacey in second period, who said that Ethan and you were spotted making out in the halls before class. Can you confirm or deny?"

"Jeez, Brie, you're too much. No, we weren't making out. No, we are not dating and no, Brie, before you ask,

I'm not gonna try to hook you up," I say, laughing as I attempt to start walking again. They don't follow and again I'm snapped back into place between them. Casey leans over and narrows her eyes at me.

"You like him though, right?"

I can feel the heat spread across my cheeks and the memory of him pressed against me as we almost kissed has my heart rate kicking up a notch.

"It's Ethan Freaking Jamison, who doesn't like him?" I say, feigning nonchalance. "Can we go to lunch now, guys? I'm starving!"

elle

I refused point blank to sit at the douche table with the rest of the jocks and the cheer squad, so we're all sitting out in the quad, the sun's beating down on my face and I'm enjoying the light breeze that's providing relief from the heat.

A phone beeps and all three of us pull out our cells.

"Mine," I chime, looking down at the screen seeing a new message from Ethan. I can't help but smile.

From: Ethan
So, considering how you turned me down for lunch and completely deflated my ego, how about meeting me after my piano practice? I need to go over some things from Hillman's class and we could grab a milkshake?
Ethan.

I type my reply while Casey and Brie stare expectantly at me.

To: Ethan
Hey,
It's a pretty big ego, I'm sure I can't have made that much of a dent. My mom's working late today, you could come over after your practice and study at my house.
I happen to make the world's best Oreo shakes ;)
B.

His reply is instant.

From: Ethan
You had me at Oreo! See u Later.
Ethan.

I put my cell away and turn to the girls. "What's with you two?"

Casey laughs. "Us two? Girl, you look like you swallowed a coat hanger, your grin is so wide. That text didn't happen to be from a certain sexy ass guitarist did it?" She wiggles her eyebrows at me. "If I didn't know better, I'd say your ass has been put on Ethan Jamison's hook 'em an fuck 'em radar."

I'm mid-sip into my water and promptly choke like a moron, coughing and spluttering, trying to regain my composure.

"Shit!" Brie sighs. "I've been trying to get on that all year."

87

"You really have no shame, huh, Brie?" I say while wiping myself down.

"You're just noticing this now?" she replies and I shake my head laughing. I should really hang out with these two more often; they're kind of hilarious.

elle

I'm in the kitchen reading when I hear a knock at the door. I rest my book on the counter and make my way to the front door. I pull it open and then just stare like a complete idiot. Ethan is standing in a pair of low slung dark jeans and a faded blue Stones t-shirt that's stretched deliciously across his chest. I'm assuming he's just showered because his hair's still damp and he smells like soap. I think I may be drooling, but to be honest, I don't care.

"You gonna invite me in?" he says with a hint of a smile.

"Sorry, yeah come in." I open the door wider and motion for him to go through to the kitchen while I take a deep breath to try and calm down before following. This boy has a serious effect on me. I walk into the kitchen and he's leaning his hip against the counter, cocky grin firmly in place.

"So, I have a confession," he says, his deep blue eyes focused intently on mine.

"Sounds ominous." I'm trying my best to not look away from his intense stare. "Go on then, enlighten me."

He pushes off the counter and stands just millimeters away from me, his chest almost touching mine; my body is instantly on high alert.

"We're alone right?"

"Yes," I answer, but it comes out as barely a whisper.

"Good."

My stomach is in knots at the anticipation of Ethan's next words. My thoughts are running away with me and all I can think of is how close he is to me, and how it's not close enough.

"So my confession," he states. "I've spent all day fantasizing about…"

My eyes widen and a smile tugs at his lips.

"Oreo milkshakes."

"Wait, what?" My confusion is written across my face and then he laughs and takes a step back. He actually laughs. What a douche.

"You're an ass!" I say, and walk over to the cupboard to retrieve two glasses. He tells me about his piano practice and makes small talk while I fix our milkshakes. He follows me up to my room so we can start studying. I'm wondering if he'll let me sit in on one of his music lessons. I can't imagine him playing the piano. I know through Em's stalking that he's supposedly stupidly gifted at it. I walk into my room and sit down Indian-style on my bed while he walks around inspecting things. He stops at my desk and moves his head forward to get a better look at my notice board. I freeze. He's in Em's stalker pictures and he's going to notice any second. Oh shit, oh shit, oh shit!

"I'm on your notice board?" he says with confusion.

"What? No you're not!" I figure the ignorance card is the one I should be playing.

"Sure I am, look," he says, pointing to the picture I took of Emily off to the side and him at his locker, clearly the main focal point.

"Oh wow, I never noticed that. Funny huh?" My acting skills suck and he must think so, too, because the look he's giving me tells me he knows I'm full of shit. I want the ground to open up and swallow me now.

"You didn't notice?" he says. "I take up two-thirds of the picture."

"Get over yourself," I say and take a drink of my milkshake, just for something to do other than worry about how much of a crazy stalker he must think I am.

He makes his way over to the bed and sits down, mirroring my pose.

"I don't have to worry about finding a little Ethan voodoo doll in here, do I?" he asks, one eyebrow lifted and his crooked grin firmly in place. I quickly place my drink on the nightstand, grab my pillow and throw it at him.

"Oh, it's on, little lady!" he shouts before I'm hit upside the head with the same pillow. The shock of the impact has me snort laughing and I reach behind me to grab more pillows for ammo. I get in a few good headshots before he grabs my arms and wrestles me onto my back as he hovers over me, panting.

"Blair," he says in a husky whisper that has my insides tightening.

I lie completely still, trying to catch my breath as his face descends. Goose bumps break out across my body and my tongue darts out to wet my lips. His eyes drop to my mouth before returning to meet my gaze. He pauses for a beat as if waiting for me to stop him. I stay completely still, willing him to kiss me and then his lips make contact with mine.

They're pressed against me so lightly that I wonder if

I'm just imagining this and then he applies a little more pressure. He starts to move his mouth and my insides feel like molten lava; an intense heat builds in the pit of my stomach and is slowly making its way south. He's supporting his weight with his elbows and cups my face with his hands, pulling me further into his kiss.

His tongue traces the seam of my mouth and when I open up to grant him access, his tongue pushes in and sweeps inside, skimming my own. A throaty groan escapes my chest and he lets his teeth nip at my lower lip before sucking it and then plunges his tongue back into my mouth. I'm aware that I'm panting and clinging to him as if he's my lifeline, but in this moment it feels like he is. I rub my legs together to relieve the pressure building between them and run my tongue against his.

This time it's his turn to moan, "Fuck me." He breathes out and it sends a wave of pleasure straight through me.

My heart's pounding so hard he can probably feel it against his chest and I run my hands down his back, slipping my fingers under the hem of his shirt, my palms flattening against his warm taught skin as I feel his muscles flexing. He pulls his lips from mine and begins a slow torturous descent, placing soft hot kisses to my jaw, neck, shoulders, then moving lower and lower until I know I'm done for.

Chapter 14

Ethan

I'M EITHER IN heaven or hell and I can't decide which: heaven because I'm kissing this amazing girl that I literally want to devour, and hell because I don't want to stop and I know I have to. I'm kissing the apex of her neck and she's making the sexiest little growls I have ever heard, it's like they have a direct line to my erection. I'm so hard it's painful; it can't be normal how turned on she makes me.

As my mouth travels lower down her chest I can feel her nipples harden beneath the fabric of her shirt. Seriously I deserve a medal for the fucking restraint I'm showing at the moment. I want to tear her clothes off, lay her bare and then taste every inch of her hot little body.

"Touch me, Ethan." Her voice is all raspy and labored, like she's fighting to breathe right. Her words have me almost coming in my jeans.

"Are you sure?" I say the words out loud and I mean them. I want this to be what she wants. If she wants me even a quarter as much as I want her, I'd die a happy man. My face is hovering over her chest, the swell of her breasts moving painfully close to my mouth with her panting. I am praying that she doesn't change her mind, when she cups my face in her hands and looks me straight in the eye.

"Please."

That's all the confirmation I need. I unbutton her shirt to expose her soft creamy flesh to me; she's wearing a purple lace bra and I can feel my body trembling with desire. She must be able to feel it too.

"Shit Blair, your perfect," I say, palming her breast and watching her eyes drift shut as her head tilts back.

I pull the material to one side and free her from its confines. Her grip on my shoulders tightens and her nails bite into my skin. Her nipple is rock hard and so ready for me, I dip my head and pull it into my mouth, sucking hard and circling the tight bud with my tongue. She lets out another tiny moan and I'm starting to really fucking panic that I'm gonna lose it. This isn't my first rodeo, I've slept with my fair share of girls but I've never felt like this before. When I've been with anyone else, I've always chased my own release; if they get off too, then good for them, but Blair's different.

I pull her nipple out of my mouth with a popping noise and move back up to kiss her again. I could do this forever and not get bored. The thought scares the shit out of me and I realize this girl fucking owns me right now. Her body arches and she pushes herself against the aching bulge in my pants; it's the sweetest torture I've ever endured.

"I want you, Ethan," she breathes in that sexy voice

of hers.

"Fuck, Princess, say that again." But she doesn't; instead, she cups her hand over my jean-clad erection and I can't think straight. My mind fogs over and all I can concentrate on is the feel of her body pressed against mine.

I run my hand down her stomach and open her jeans.

"Is this okay?" I ask, if she says no I think I may actually cry. She nods her approval and I slip my hand down over her panties cupping her, I can feel her heat radiating against my hand. I press my mouth to hers and run my tongue across her lips.

She cries out, whimpering and kicking her legs out straight tensing them. I look down, smiling at the effect I seem to be having on her as I run my nose against her cheek inhaling her sweet scent. I slip my hand under the waistband of the panties and she bucks on the bed.

"Wait," she moans, and I freeze instantly.

I pull away, worried that I've overstepped the mark, that I've read the signals wrong and this isn't what she wants, but I'm put at ease as she raises her ass off the bed and shimmies out of her jeans, tossing them on the floor beside her.

"You're so damn hot," I tell her as I position myself between her legs and hook my fingers over her panties, slowly pulling them down. I kiss the inside of both her thighs and it's as much as I can take.

"I need to taste you, Princess."

"Oh god, Ethan, please I…"

Before she can finish speaking I move to the edge of her bed and drop to my knees, pulling her towards me and I press my mouth to her core.

She gasps and takes in a sharp breath as her whole

body goes rigid for a second before she exhales and murmurs something unintelligible.

"I got you, Princess…just relax," I say against her as I trace her seam with my tongue and suckle on her clit. Shit, she tastes so sweet.

I circle, flick, lick and repeat as she's thrashing about under me. I slide a finger inside of her and then I'm thrusting it in and out while carrying on with my assault on her clit. I don't stop until she's exploding around me and her whole body is trembling. Somewhere along the way she's lost her glasses and her hair's a wild mess across the bed sheets.

"Fuck me…you're beautiful," I tell her, adjusting my cock that feels like a bomb about to detonate at any second. I move to stand and she grabs the back of my legs, pulling me back down onto her.

"That was wow… just wow," she says and kisses me, sucking my tongue into her mouth. God, this girl couldn't be any sexier.

"I don't think I've ever wanted anyone as much as I want you," I whisper into her neck. "Can I keep you?"

She pulls back and smiles at me, it lights up her whole face, those huge green eyes sparkling at me. This is it, I realize. The moment I know I would rather die than spend another second without her.

"You're amazing Blair, I'm kinda crazy for you."

I need her to know how I feel. To know that she's not just some random hook up. I want her to know that she's it for me. I just need her.

"I'm so far past crazy for you," she whispers.

I exhale in relief, and pull her into a tight embrace.

The comfort of those few words filling my whole body with a sense of peace, Like she's a piece of me that I never knew was missing. She completes me, makes me feel whole.

"Do you...um, should I?" she says, pulling away and diverting her eyes to my dick that is straining against my pants.

I let my amusement at her awkward suggestion show on my face. I wink and lean forward kissing her forehead. "That's nothing a cold shower or ten won't take care of."

There's nothing more in this moment I want than to be inside of her, but when it happens, I don't want it to be some rush job before her mom gets home from work.

I release my hold of her and sit on the bed watching as she pulls her panties back into place and steps back into her jeans.

She turns to face me with a look of confusion covering her pretty little face.

"What?" I ask.

She moves forward and stands between my legs looking down at me.

I lift my eyebrows and wait as she decides how to say whatever it is that she's wanting to.

"I just want to know...this is embarrassing, I mean, I'm not the type of girl that hooks up and does this kind of thing, you know? I've never done this and I, um...I just need to know what this is. What are we doing?"

She's shaking as I reach up and grab her waist, pulling her down onto my lap.

"You're so fucking cute when you're awkward," I tell her. "And this," I motion with my finger between us, "this is me, making you mine."

Chapter 15

Blair

IT'S BEEN ONE whole week since Ethan and I started dating. At least I think that's what we're doing. I asked him after the 'tutoring session' that had nothing to do with learning math and everything to do with learning each other. His response turned me into a puddle; he's the complete opposite of everything I expected him to be. I assumed that our relationship in school would pretty much stay the same.

He has a reputation for being a man-whore and his actions generally confirmed it. The last thing I expected was for him to be the attentive boyfriend type, the one who opens doors and carries books and blows off the guys to eat lunch with me outside. It's only been a week and I'm wondering if the novelty of this for him will wear off. He's told me he's never been in a relationship before, or rather he's never been exclusive with anyone. He knows I've never had a relationship—period—so I can't help thinking that the wheels are gonna fall off this thing. I'm pretty sure that when they do he'll have ruined me. I literally can't go more than a couple of hours without thinking about him. I've turned into a complete sappy mess.

The first day at school with Ethan and me as a couple was the weirdest day ever. It's like dating a member of Kickstart has qualified me to be socially accepted by the cheer squad, which, apart from Casey and Brie, are a bunch of airheads whose main objective is to climb the popularity ladder and date a band member or the next best thing, a jock.

The fact that they're being nice to me freaks me out and is about as genuine as Nicki Minaj's chest. Drew's girlfriend Dannii seems nice but there's something about her that's a little off, I'm just not sure what. The guys all seem cool; Jackson is hilarious, I like him a lot. And apparently so does Brie, now that Ethan's off the market.

"Hey Princess, loving your shirt this morning," Ethan greets as I climb out of my car at school.

I look down to remind myself which shirt I'm actually wearing, and realize it's the Pi one I wore that first day in the library.

"Are you staring at my chest, Jamison?" I ask in mock disgust.

"I'm allowed to ogle your breasts now, you're mine," he says, winking and pulling me into his side, kissing my temple.

"So romantic," I sigh and shake my head but I can't keep the goofy smile off my face.

"So, Sam, our manager, lined a gig up for us tomorrow night. It's at a pretty cool club in town; the band they had booked bailed so we've got the spot. I was wondering if you wanted to come."

I've only seen a few live bands before, and they've always been with Em. We did attempt to go see Kickstart play once at the beginning of the year, but it was smoky and overcrowded. Emily felt ill and we left just as the band came on. She was there for Ethan rather than the music, so once she'd caught a glimpse of him she admitted defeat and we left before she passed out. It's weird how things turn out. I still feel a little guilty that I'm with him and can't help wondering if she'd be okay with us. I think she would, but I'd give anything for her to be able to tell me that in person. I miss talking to her, or rather I miss being talked at by her. The thought makes my chest ache and I have a sudden overwhelming urge to cry.

"You look like I just ran over your cat, not asked you to come listen to us play. You don't have to come if you don't want to," he says noticing the look on my face.

"What? Oh, it's not that, of course I'll come. I've only ever been to a few gigs and they were with Emily; you asking just made me think of her, is all."

"I'm sorry, Princess," he says, stopping and pulling me into his chest tightly. His strong arms pin me in place and I close my eyes for a second, my ear pressed to his chest listening to the steady beat of his heart.

His chin is resting on top of my head and I want to stand like this forever, enveloped in his warmth.

"Yo, dickhead!" TJ's voice breaks the moment and Ethan pulls back, looking at me, "You okay?" he asks, and I nod and smile my reply.

"E, man, how's it going?" TJ asks, coming up beside us as we make our way into the building.

"Hey Blair," he flashes me a smile and turns back to Ethan.

"We're good, you?"

"Better once we've nailed the new set list tomorrow night."

They do the weird first bump thing guys do and then carry on talking music until we reach the halls and need to separate for different classes.

"Meet you at lunch," Ethan says, kissing me quickly on the cheek and then disappearing around the corner with TJ as I make my way to my first period Lit class.

$$\mathcal{ele}$$

I'd spoken to Ethan before heading out to the club and he'd instructed me to wait for him once Kickstart's set ended so we could go grab something to eat. I'm sitting at a table a couple rows from the stage watching the guys cast their magic. Drew has a great voice but Ethan's is so good, like ridiculously good. I can't take my eyes off of him. His body's glistening with sweat as his fingers are moving frantically over his guitar and his eyes are closed tightly as he sings the lyrics into the mic. It looks so natural to him, like he was born doing this. The crowed goes nuts as he finishes the song and opens his eyes. I jump up cheering, getting caught up in the atmosphere. I want to melt as he scans the crowed for my face, finds it and then winks at me. Every time he does it I get goose bumps. It's so cocky but totally sexy and he knows it. I take my seat again as someone comes to sit beside me a little too close for comfort, I turn to see Della smirking at me. Great!

"Hey it's Blair, isn't it?" she asks.

"Um…yeah, hi."

"So, how're things with Ethan?" As soon as the words leave her lips I want to get up and leave. I know this isn't going to end well, it's written all over her overly made-up smug face.

"Fine, thanks," I clip out, hoping like hell she'll just get up and leave. No such luck.

"You know, it's not going to last, right?"

What a bitch!

"Sorry, why's that?" I ask, trying to feign nonchalance in my tone.

"He doesn't do exclusivity. You should know that. Everyone does, I'm the closest he's gotten to a relationship and when he's finished toying around with you he'll be back. He always comes back." She's smiling at me and it's sickly sweet.

I've never been in a fight before but I can see that changing real fast; I want to rip this girl's head off. But it's not me—I'm the quiet one, I run from awkward situations and that's what I'm about to do until she lets out a satisfied little laugh. Like she knows she's just upset me and she's won.

"I'm sorry, can you die from constipation?" She gives me a blank look and I continue. "I'm just a little concerned about how full of shit you are. There is no way in hell he'll be going near you again."

I'm so mad I can feel heat radiating off of me as I clench my fists at my side, trying to stay calm. I stand and make to move past her when she grabs my arm and gets in my face.

"I wouldn't be too sure about that. I know Ethan a whole lot better than you think. I bet he doesn't even call you by your name when you're screwing, does he? Let me guess, he calls you 'babe' or 'doll' or another pet name you probably think is fucking adorable. Wanna know why? Because that way he doesn't have to remember your name, sweetheart, especially when he's thinking about someone else."

I can feel my eyes starting to sting with the tears that I'd rather die than let this bitch see fall.

"You're pathetic," I practically spit, shrugging out of her hold. But there's no fire behind my words this time because I'm the one who feels pathetic. He calls me 'princess' and I loved it up until two seconds ago. I feel sick and I feel stupid. A leopard doesn't change its spots; I'm a smart girl, I should know this.

"No, honey, you're the pathetic one thinking you had anything with him. You do know he calls you the 'tutor nerd' to his friends, right? Doesn't sound like a guy in love to me."

I take a deep breath and barge my way past her, weaving in and out of the tables. I reach the exit doors and look back just in time to see the look of confusion cross Ethan's face as he notices me about to leave. I don't mean to make eye contact but I do and it feels like someone has punched me in the stomach and ripped my heart out. He's a singer and guitarist in a band. Mr. Popularity and me…I'm nobody. What was I thinking? I'm grateful that I haven't slept with him yet.

The band is still playing and Ethan's singing, but he knows something's wrong, he can see it written all over me. My poker face officially sucks. He stops singing midsong, pulls his guitar strap over his head and places it down on the stage. There's confusion on everyone's faces as they wonder what the fuck he's doing, Drew picks up where Ethan left off and the guys carry on but I can hear a man shouting his name. I spin and push the doors open and break into a run across the parking lot. I don't want him to catch up to me, I don't want him to see me cry; in fact, right now I don't want to see him ever again.

I reach the end of the lot just as I hear my name echo through the quiet. I don't stop, though. I run past a few more vehicles and head for my car. I grab the door handle just as he catches me and cages me against the door with his arms.

"What's happened, what's wrong?" he's out of breath and his eyes are frantically searching my face.

"Move, Ethan."

"What…no, Princess, what's wrong? Why ar—"

"Don't fucking call me that!" I attempt to push him back from me but he stays where he is, like a mountain of steel that I couldn't move if my life depended on it.

I can't hold back anymore and I feel hot tears spill onto my cheeks. He pulls back slightly but grabs onto my shoulders, there's panic written across his absurdly pretty face.

"Fuck Blair, tell me what happened."

"Why don't you go ask Della Fucking Fields!" I sob and I hate that he's seeing this. I hate that I'm being weak and can't confront him about this without him knowing how much pain I'm in.

"I don't want to ask her anything, I'm asking you."

"Fine." I straighten my back and stand tall. "Where

do I start? Oh yeah, that's right…she told me why you call me Princess, the same reason you call everyone you hook up with babe or whatever, so you don't have to remember their names." I pause for a beat to see his reaction but he just stands looking blankly at me so I continue. "But you don't just call me 'Princess', do you asshole? No, you call me the 'tutor nerd' to all your friends. God I'm a fucking idiot, I knew yo—"

"Stop! Shit, Blair, just stop for a minute. I referred to you as tutor nerd before I knew who the fuck you were," he says, looking me straight in the eye. "I got your number from Hillman but never got your name. I don't call you that now. As for why I call you Princess. Shit, I can't believe this. I call you Princess because that's what you are to me, not because I can't be bothered remember your fucking name. Jesus, Blair."

I'm taking in what he's saying but the crying has made me all foggy and my glasses have misted up. I pull them off and go to wipe them on the hem of my shirt. He grabs a hold of my wrists and bends at the knee to bring his face level with mine.

"Don't let her do this Blair, please. You know me, you're the only person that does! Yeah, I've been a dick in the past but you're different. I'm different with you."

There's desperation in his voice and I can't process this right now. I'm a mess and I just want to leave. I turn and attempt to open my car door again, but his arms are around me in an instant, pulling my back against his chest. He places his head on my shoulder so his sweat-dampened cheek is pressed against mine.

"Don't do this, don't walk away from me Blair." His voice quivers and he pulls me tighter to him. "Not over this." He's holding me like I'm about to disappear and I realize that I could never walk away from him.

He's woven a spell over me. I take a deep breath and consider his explanation; I slowly feel my resolve break when I realize that I somehow know it's the truth.

I twist in his embrace and bury my face into his chest, wrapping my arms around his waist and pressing as close to him as I can get.

"I'm not going anywhere," I say into his shirt as I feel him exhale a long breath.

"Promise me," he says so quietly I barely hear it.

"I promise."

Chapter 16

Ethan

I'M SHAKING, THERE'S an insane amount of adrenaline cursing through my veins and I can feel my heart slamming against my chest so hard that I'm sure I'm about to have a heart attack. Blair's pressed against me, holding my waist as I will myself to relax and calm down. She's not going anywhere, even if she wanted to I can't let her— I won't let her. She may not realize it yet but I've given her my heart and I'm not about to accept it back. It comes with a no-return policy, She owns it; she owns me. As much as that thought scares me it's the only thing that keeps me grounded. She's what makes me want to wake up in a morning. I feel like a junkie and Blair's my fix; I can't operate or function without her and I don't ever want to try.

I cup her face in my hands and shakily bring her lips to mine. I kiss her softly, savoring the feeling of her, trying to commit the taste of her mouth to my memory. She lets out a tiny moan and I can't help but increase the pressure of the kiss. I pull away and rest my forehead against hers in relief that she's not running from me. The club doors fling open and Sam's booming voice slices through the atmosphere shattering the stillness of the moment.

"JAMISON! WHAT THE HELL ARE YOU DO-ING?"

Blair winces and looks at me wide-eyed. I squeeze her hand before dropping it and turning to see our manager storming towards me looking more pissed off than I think I've ever seen him.

"UNLESS YOU'RE DYING, GET YOUR ASS BACK ON THAT STAGE NOW!" he's screaming at me and his shaved head is as red as the rest of his angry-looking face.

"Sorry boss, I'm coming," I say, walking towards him. He promptly turns and heads back inside as I motion for Blair to follow me.

"I'll wait for you in my car," she says, biting her lip. "I can't face going back in there just yet."

"Are you sure? Please don't just leave as soon as I'm back inside." I know I sound needy as fuck but I don't care.

"I already told you…I'm not going anywhere. I'll be right here when you come back out." She gives me a sad smile and I feel like a complete prick for leaving here out here on her own, but if I don't get back in there I'll be in the shit with the guys. Sam's working his ass off promot-ing us and getting us gigs, and the guys are convinced he can get us signed. Me, I'm not so sure, and it doesn't really matter. As long as my scholarship works out, I'm out of here, band or no band.

"Okay, Princess," I wince as the words leave my mouth and she notices. I jog back to where she's standing and kiss her forehead.

"Sorry." She pulls my face down and presses her mouth to mine. "You can call me Princess," she says against my lips, and I know I need to get my ass back into the club, but right now wherever she is, is the only place I want to be.

elle

I step back into the club and am promptly pulled to the side by Sam.

"I want you to come and see me first thing tomorrow morning," he says, his eyes still glued to the stage watching the guys play. "Make sure you show up, don't fuck up everyone else's chance of being signed, Ethan. I have some things I need to go through with you."

"I'll be there." I'm not about to miss that meeting. If I get dropped from the band it's no big deal to me, but I can't be responsible for screwing up the rest of the guys' opportunities. It's not fair to them.

When the gig is finally over I tell Blair to follow me back to my house, My dad's working nights again so it's just my mom home. I tell her we can order pizza and watch a movie in the pool house. She agrees and fifteen minutes later she's pulling up behind me in my drive. She gets out and walks to the front door where I'm standing with my hand out for her waiting. She takes it and looks a little nervous.

"I need to check in on my mom and let her know I'm home. Come meet her." I lead her into the family room. Mom's reading and places her book down to stand up as she sees me walk in, hand in hand with Blair.

She quickly smoothes out her shocked face and replaces it with a huge smile as she moves forward to greet us.

"Mom, this is Blair, my girlfriend," I say. "Blair this is my mom, Moira."

I don't know who looks more startled that I introduced her as my "girlfriend"—Blair or my mom. There's an awkward silence for a few beats before my mom finally recovers.

"Blair, it's so nice to meet you," she says, pulling her in for a quick hug.

"It's lovely to meet you, too, Mrs. Jamison."

"Hush now, Mrs. Jamison is my mother in-law. Call me Moira."

Blair offers her a warm smile and I squeeze her hand slightly, trying to ease her obvious nerves.

"We're ordering pizza and watching a movie in the pool house," I tell Mom over my shoulder as I motion Blair out of the room.

ele

I'm sitting on the floor with my back resting against the futon and Blair's leaning back against my chest as we eat pizza and watch Reservoir Dogs. I told her to pick the film and was fully expecting her to pick some girly shit. Turns out her taste in movies are just another thing to add to my list of awesome things about my girl.

"Ugh…I'm stuffed," she says, throwing the crust of her pizza back into the open box.

She rests her head back against me and gives me a perfect view straight down her shirt. I can't move my gaze; it feels like my eyes have been glued to her. I mesmerized watching how her breathing expands and lifts her chest. I feel myself harden instantly against her back and she obviously does too, because she starts to subtly grind her ass back into me. Heat floods my body as the blood rushes straight to my dick. I take a deep breath of her sweet perfume and my mind is instantly in the gutter. I'm picturing all the things I want to do to her sexy little body, all the places I want to taste. I feel dizzy with want and desire. This girl does something to my body, it's like she's kryptonite and I'm powerless to stop the effect she has on me. Her cell starts to ring, tearing me from my thoughts as she moves forward to grab it.

"Hey, Mom," she answers, as I stand and excuse myself to the bathroom to adjust my hard-on.

I return a minute later and Blair's standing with her jacket and sneakers on and her purse thrown over her shoulder. I sigh internally that she's going to leave; I had a whole scenario of things I wanted to do with her tonight that has just been squashed.

"I should get going," she says as she steps forward and kisses me lightly.

I grab her waist and pull her hard into me, my dick immediately starting to twitch again.

"Do you have to?" I plead with my eyes but she just smiles and steps back again.

"Afraid so, slick." She fakes a pout. "I have a ton of

homework and I've barley seen or spoken to my mom all week. I need to check in."

I sigh and begin to walk her out to her car.

"What's your plans for this weekend, baby?" I ask as she opens her car door and tosses her purse inside. "Whatever they are they'd better include me," I tell her, lifting my eyebrow and giving her a pointed look.

"No plans yet—what do you wanna do?"

I wiggle my eyebrows at her and she laughs and slaps my chest playfully.

"Perv!"

"Yeah, and you love it," I retort, and her face flashes an emotion I've not seen before.

"I have an idea but it's kind of embarrassing," she says, looking down at her sneakers. I lift her chin and smile.

"You don't ever have to be embarrassed about anything in front of me, Princess."

She lets out a little laugh and meets my gaze.

"Okay, well, I kind of want to cross of another thing from Em's list," she says eyeing me warily. "Let's just say it involves a large expanse of water and not very many clothes."

I feel my jaw fall open and I silently thank the hell out of Emily in my head. I didn't know the girl but right now I fucking love her.

"You wanna go skinny dipping?" I ask, my voice laced with hope.

Her cheeks redden instantly as she nods and I mentally high-five Emily.

"Fuck yeah, I'm up for that!" I lean in and kiss her

forehead as she gets into her car.

"See you at school tomorrow." I step back as she reverses out the drive and then watch her tail lights disappear down the road. All of a sudden I can't wait for this weekend. I head back up to the house and walk into the kitchen to grab a soda. Mom's doing the dishes and turns to look at my with an eyebrow raised.

"What?" I ask her, smiling because I already know what's coming.

"Girlfriend, huh? She seems like a nice girl. I was a little surprised you haven't mentioned her before now, though."

I take a long pull on my soda before answering her.

"It's a new thing. We've only been together a week."

"Pretty quick to be introducing her to us then, especially since you've never brought any of your other girlfriends to meet us," Mom says still smiling at me.

"Yeah well, I've never had a girlfriend to introduce before."

"So you really like this girl then?" she asks, cocking her head, the question clear in her voice.

My mind quickly answers, 'no I don't really like this girl, I'm pretty sure I love her'. I'm startled by my own thoughts and look back to Mom who's watching me with a knowing grin spreading across her face.

"Yeah, you could say that," is all I can respond before quickly making my way out of the kitchen to go sort my head out. A week isn't long enough to be falling in love with someone, I tell myself. It can't be love; it's probably just lust. But even as I'm thinking it, I know I'm full of crap. I just don't dare admit it.

Chapter 17

Blair

I'M A MASS of nerves and tension as Saturday afternoon finally arrives. I'm wringing my hands together and bouncing my knees nervously, sitting on the porch waiting for Ethan to pick me up. Mom headed into town to do some shopping about thirty minutes ago. She asked what I had planned today and I'd told her that Ethan and I were going to the beach.

Technically it's true so I'm not lying to her, I've just chosen to omit the part about skinny dipping...Mom doesn't know about Em's list and truthfully, if she did, I don't think she'd want me to carry out Emily's requests. My mother is a firm believer that you should live your life as your own, and not be pulled into situations that you're not completely happy with. I wish she could take her own advice sometimes.

I told her about Ethan and I dating on Thursday evening when I arrived home. She seemed really happy for me, but when I'd told her that Emily was practically in love with him and I felt guilty, she sat me down and we had a real mother daughter heart-to-heart. She told me that Em would most likely be happy that I ended up with him rather than someone else, and that I shouldn't let the past dictate my future. Emily was gone and Ethan and I were not. I'd forgotten how good my mom was at the mother daughter talks. She has definitely helped to ease the feeling of guilt a little.

I'm busying myself with my e-reader when Ethan finally pulls on to the drive. He's in a 4x4 with two bicycles hooked up on the back. He jumps out and flashes me a crooked grin, my insides immediately turn to lava. The boy is H.O.T.

"Ready for some swimming, Princess?" He smirks, making his way over to kiss me. He wraps his arms around my waist, cupping my ass with his hands.

"Hey, handsome. Nice ride." I motion to the Range Rover he pulled up in and he laughs.

"Yeah, I couldn't get the bikes on my Camaro, so Mom let me use her car."

"Um…I thought we were going to the beach?" I grab the beach bag I packed and dangle it in front of him.

"Change of plan. I know a great trail we can take the bikes on. It just so happens there's a great little secluded part of a lake at the end where we can swim." His eyes roam down my body slowly and then return back to my face, looking like they want to eat me, and I narrow my eyes and give him a look.

"What?" he asks, his eyes wide and innocent looking. "You look hot; surely I'm allowed to appreciate the view."

I laugh and nudge his shoulder with my own as I

gather up my stuff to put in the car.

"Plus if you didn't want me looking at you like that, you should have worn something different, Princess."

I look down and assess what I'm wearing: a bright green tank and a pair of denim cut-off shorts over my plain black bikini and, of course, my Chucks. I look back at him, confused, and he lets out a deep throaty laugh.

"You have no idea how sexy you are, do you? I love it," he says, before boosting me up into the seat of the Range Rover.

A flush takes over my body and I break out in goose bumps at the contact. I wonder if it's normal to feel like this from such an innocent touch; I have a suspicion that I'm always going to react this way around him.

We drive a little way out of Santa Maria before I ask where he's taking me exactly. Oso Flaco Lake is his reply. I've lived my whole life in Santa Maria and have never been.

We drive for about a half an hour, listening to music in a comfortable silence before we finally park and Ethan gets the bikes as I grab our bags from the backseat.

I heft his backpack up over my shoulder and it feels like he's smuggling rocks in there.

"Jeez, what did you pack in your bag?" I shout out. "It weighs more than me!"

He appears at my side with a dazzling smile plastered across his face. "You'll see."

We take the bikes and cycle for about twenty minutes down little trails that are flanked by pretty blue and yellow wildflowers. The heat's just starting to get to me when Ethan stops.

"This will do," he says and points to a shaded area of grass just off the trail. I dismount the bike as ladylike as I can manage, but the last time I cycled I was about ten years old and my ass is already starting to ache from the seat. We lean the bikes up against a huge tree and I lift my eyebrow at him.

"What now?" I ask, smoothing my hair away from my face.

"Now we eat," he says, pulling a blanket from the top of his backpack and laying it out across the grass. He tosses two bottles of water in my direction and then comes to sit next to me, handing me a brown paper bag with a sandwich, apple and chips inside.

"I can't cook for shit but I make a mean packed lunch." He grins at me and I want to toss the lunch aside and just feast on him. He's so freaking adorable.

"You made me lunch? You're full of surprises," I tell him and pull out my sandwich. "Peanut butter and jelly? What are we, five?" I say, laughing.

"Only the best for my woman." He grins and I melt a little more. His woman.

We finish eating and make our way on foot through a few trees, coming out onto a sand bank. There's a huge wooden dock stretching out across the water and it's breathtaking.

"Ready to cross another item off your list?" he asks, and I'm suddenly nervous as hell. It obviously shows on my face because Ethan looks down at me and takes my hand.

"You don't have to do this, you know. We can just swim in our suits and have fun." His voice is tender and calming and it's all the encouragement I need.

My fingers grip the hem of my tank and I pull it over my head, dropping it at my feet. Ethan's eyes widen for a second before he mirrors my action and removes his own shirt.

I watch in a trance as his muscles flex with his movements and I run my eyes greedily over the dips in his abs. He straightens and waits, taking his cues from me.

I hook my thumbs into the waistband of my shorts and shimmy them down my legs, never once taking my eyes from his. He smiles and then like before, he mirrors my actions and does the same. I'm standing in my black bikini staring at the sight of Ethan in just a pair of black boxer briefs.

"Where are your swim shorts?" I ask him and he lets out a gruff laugh.

"I didn't pack them, Blair; didn't think I'd need them." He's eyeing me carefully and I can feel the blush spreading across my face and neck like wildfire.

"Oh," Is all I can manage.

He moves forward and takes my hand, leading me out onto the dock. We're completely alone and the sun is bouncing off the surface of the water, making it shimmer and look like a sea of diamonds laid out before us.

"To hell with it," I say and Ethan looks at me, confused. "Go big or go home, right?" I flash him a smile as I pull the tie at the back of my neck and let the two triangles covering my chest fall to the floor.

His eyes widen and he stands staring at me like I've just grown another head. I instantly feel self-conscious and cover myself with my arms.

"Oh no you don't," he smiles, lunging forward and

picking me up, tossing me over his shoulder as he runs to the end of the dock. I'm screaming and giggling as he leaps off and plunges us both into the frigid-cold water.

We break the surface and I feel as though I've been stabbed with a thousand tiny knives as the water bites at my skin.

"Fuck, that's cold!" he gasps as I'm trying to catch my breath.

"No shit!" I deadpan treading water.

"You said go big or go home," he laughs then reaches down into the water. His hand emerges a second later with his boxers firm in its grip. He tosses them onto the dock and then turns back to me with a questioning smirk.

I figure he can't see my body under the water too well so I do the same and his grin is instant.

"I would have bet money that you were gonna chicken out," he laughs, shaking his head and swimming closer to me. He pulls me into his hard body and my legs instinctively wrap around his waist, my arms circling his neck.

He leans forward and kisses me like I'm about to disappear, urgent and hard, and I let out an involuntary moan and tighten my grip on him. Our lips are fused together and I lick the inside of his mouth, tangling my tongue with his. I slide my arms from around his neck, down his chest and under the water, bringing them around his back and digging my fingers into the taut skin.

"Fuck, Blair, you feel so good." He's palming my ass and raining kisses across my jaw and down my neck.

The kisses leave fire in their wake and my whole body is instantly on high alert. I grind myself into his waist shamelessly, trying to create friction and ease the building ache between my legs. I can feel his erection pressed against my stomach and I can't concentrate on anything else. I want him. I really want him. We've been together a week and I know it's not long enough to be throwing myself at him like this, but the feelings he elicits are so intense I can't stop.

I feel like I could combust at any second. I've held on to my virginity for eighteen years without ever really considering giving it to anyone. Ethan's been in my life two minutes and I'm literally trying to throw it at him. I need to calm down, slow down, and gather my thoughts. He mumbles how good I taste against my collarbone and it sends a wave of desire straight through me.

"You're shivering like crazy," he says, pulling his head back with a look of concern.

I know it has more to do with being naked and pressed up against each other than the fact that the lake is cold as hell, but I don't want to seem like a complete moron.

"Well, duh…the water's freaking freezing!" I clip out and he immediately starts to swim the few meters back to the dock, dragging me through the water with him.

"Come on, let's get out and get you warm."

I pout and regret telling him I was cold. I was really enjoying being wrapped around him.

He drops my hand and uses both of his to propel himself out of the water and on to the dock. Naked! My eyes are like saucers as I watch the water race down his tanned broad back, dipping into the dimples at its base and then the droplets make their way over his amazing ass. I must have stopped treading water at some point while perving on Ethan because I sink. I break the surface again flailing my arms and legs about, coughing and spluttering.

Ethan turns and drops to his knees, leaning over the side and grabbing my arm to pull me up.

Now I have a perfect view of absolutely everything and I gasp at the sight of him naked and hard—and huge. The water's freezing and it doesn't seem to have had any type of effect on him.

"Babe, stop splashing around and grab my hand, I'll pull you up."

I reach out to take a hold of him and then pull my arm quickly away.

"No! I'm naked!" I screech.

His lips pull up at the side into a crooked grin and his dimples appear full force. "I'm aware of that," he says in a low gravelly voice.

"I'm not getting out while you can see me; turn around."

He breaks into laughter and stands back up, not bothering to try and shield himself from my view.

"No fair, Princess, you got to see me," he says, still laughing.

The sight of him transfixes me. He's prefect. The water is making his body glisten and I can't pull my eyes away from the deep-cut V that's leading down to where I'm desperately trying not to look.

"Yeah, well, I'm not the exhibitionist that you are, so turn around, and no peeking."

"Kill joy." He winks and then turns and literally struts down the dock with his back to me. Cocky asshole, I think to myself. But my smile is huge.

Chapter 18

Ethan

I DROVE BLAIR home from the lake and told her that I'd call her later; I needed to get the car back to my mom and I still had a ton of homework to get through. It wasn't strictly a lie—I do have those things to do—but I knew that if I spent any more time with her at the lake, there was no way I could have controlled myself. I want to sleep with this girl more than I want my next breath. If she were anyone else I'd have tried my luck in the water as she was grinding her hot little body against mine. She's not just anybody, though, and I'm not about to take her virginity at the lake where anyone could have walked by. I park the car and walk into the house to return the keys. Mom and Dad are sitting at the island drinking coffee and reading; Mom, her book and Dad, the newspaper.

"It's about time you showed up," Dad says, peering over the top of the paper at me as I cross the kitchen and toss the car keys on to the counter.

"Sorry, didn't realize I was supposed to be home for anything," I tell him, opening the fridge and retrieving a bottle of water.

"Had an interesting little chat earlier with Sam Jones." He lifts his eyebrow and stares at me, waiting for my response.

My stomach bottoms out and I pause with the water at my lips.

"Yeah, he told me about the little stunt you pulled— leaving in the middle of a set on Friday." Shit. I draw the bottle away from my mouth and place it on the counter without taking a drink. Mom's shooting me a look with her eyes that's pleading with me silently, 'please don't make him angry', but what the hell am I supposed to do? He's always fucking angry.

"I can explain, I—" I manage to stammer out before he interrupts.

"Damn right you'd better explain. You know what else Sam mentioned? He told me all about the audition he's set up for the band to go play in front of some sup-posedly big shot music execs. The guy's delusional, and so are you if you think it will lead to anything. What the hell is that all about, huh? You have a music scholarship you need to secure; you can't be fucking around with this band, Ethan. It's already gonna cost your mamma and me a for-tune to send you to Eastman since you couldn't pull your lazy ass finger out and get a full scholarship. You have to bleed us dry because you couldn't be bothered to study hard enough." I tense as his words hit their mark and he continues.

"You're such a screw up, Ethan, Now instead of sav-ing for our retirement, we have to put you through fucking college. I managed to get a scholarship and support myself through school. But then again, I'm not a lazy little fucker who expects everything handed to him on a goddamn plate, am I?"

Mom scrapes her chair back against the hardwood and walks over to my father, placing her hand on his shoulder.

"Calm down Frank, let him explain," she says in a weak timid voice, but her attempt at calming the situation falls on deaf ears.

He shrugs her hand from his shoulder and comes to a stand himself. He looks twice as pissed now, the anger practically rolling off him.

"Don't try to turn this on me, Moira." he bites out, taking four large strides and stopping inches from my face.

"I'm sorry, sir. I won't let the band interfere with Eastman," I mutter, trying to diffuse his mood as quickly as possible.

"Sorry doesn't fucking cut it!" he screams in my face, pushing me back so I slam into the refrigerator. I chance a quick look over to my mom but she's in the doorway with her head held low.

"Don't be fucking looking at her for help, you little son of a bitch. Act like a man."

I'm about to speak when he delivers a swift blow to my stomach; the force of the impact knocks the air from my lungs and I slump forward gasping for a breath. My chest is on fire and I can't get any oxygen as I try to straighten.

His rage is palpable as he pounds his fists into my side. I want to shout out in pain, but there's no fucking way on earth I would give him that satisfaction, so I do as I always do—I stand unmoving and just take it. Punch after punch into the same agonizing spot on my ribs, and all the while he's telling me I'm a sorry little shit that's nothing but a noose around his neck.

I switch off and go into a daze; my body is here in the kitchen yet my mind's with Blair. I'm picturing her pretty face and those beautiful big green eyes hidden under her glasses. I suddenly realize that the blows don't seem to be coming with the same strength now; he must be getting tired. Finally, he relents and stalks out the backdoor, slamming it so loud it sounds as if it's about to fall from its hinges. I struggle to straighten and lean my head against the refrigerator, holding my side and taking painful shallow breaths. I look up in time to see my mom hurrying towards me; she grabs my arm, pulling it around her shoulders, and moves me over to the bar stools to sit down.

"Do you need an ice pack, honey?" she asks, her voice trembling and a sadness in her eyes that tells me she's sorry.

"I'm fine," I bite out. and I can't help but sound harsh. I'm not the one who just stood watching while my husband beat the shit out of my kid for no good fucking reason. He didn't even give me a chance to explain this time. I stagger to my feet and make my way over to the door. "I'll be in my room," I huff without looking back.

"You want me to bring you anything?" she asks and I shake my head as I make my way down the hall. I don't want anything from her, I think as I navigate the stairs in pain.

I lie on my bed staring at the ceiling. I only need to make it until graduation, then I'm out of here. If I didn't need help with college I'd have left before now. I'm tired and sore, my ribs ache with every breath I take and I feel pretty fucking low. I pull my cell from my pocket and my thumb hovers over Blair's name. I'm having an internal battle about what to say to her. I have the urge to call and tell her what happened, just for a chance to vent out all the shit that's running through my mind; it would be a weight off my shoulders, but I don't want to transfer the burden.

I toss my phone down and close my eyes, willing sleep to come. I manage about fifteen minutes before I decide that this is bullshit and get up, grab my phone, and make my way outside to my car. I'm on autopilot; I don't remember the drive but ten minutes later I'm sitting opposite Blair's house. The light is on in her bedroom and her car's in the drive so I know she's home. I sit with the car idling at the curb like some weird creeper watching her house. She walks past the window and seeing her I make up my mind. I'm out of my car and knocking at her front door before I have chance to talk myself out of it.

"Ethan! Miss me so much you're back already?" she asks, smiling at me. She's changed out of her bikini and shorts and is wearing lounge pants and a tank top with her hair falling loose around her shoulders. She moves forward to kiss me, lacing her arms around me and I wince from the pain that shoots across my chest.

Her eyes widen and I can practically see the cogs turning in her mind before it dawns on her why I'm in pain.

"Hey Princess, can I come in?"

"Course, babe. Are you okay? What's happened?" she asks with a concerned frown marring her features.

"The asshole strikes again," I tell her with a laugh, attempting to make light of the situation as she walks me through the house and up to her room.

"Where's your mom?"

"Out with her friend, Clare," she answers. I'm led into her room and down onto her bed as she sits facing me Indian-style.

"How badly has he hurt you? Do you need me to go and get you some pain meds?" Her face looks completely gutted and I instantly hate myself for putting that look there.

"I'm fine, it's not too painful." I run the back of my fingers down her soft pink cheeks and her eyes drift closed from the contact. She takes my hand in both of hers and squeezes it slightly.

"I'm glad you're here," she says and my shoulders relax. I exhale a deep breath and meet her eyes.

"I only ever want to be where you are," I tell her, and it's the truth. She doesn't know it, but she brings me a peace I never knew existed.

Chapter 19

Blair

THREE WEEKS HAVE passed since the night Ethan turned up on my doorstep battered and bruised from his own father's hands. I told him I thought it was time to tell someone about what was happening, but just like last time, he shot me down and told me he had it under control. Now every time I touch him, I'm subtly looking for any signs that he's wincing or tensing in pain. He's told me that he hasn't had any further run-ins with his dad and I believe him, but it doesn't stop me from checking. It's a messed up situation and one that I hate knowing that I'm doing absolutely nothing about.

I've never been the type of person to not speak up when I see something wrong happening. Yeah, I may be quiet and shy away from people, but I know right from wrong. Well, at least I used to. What kind of a girlfriend knows that her boyfriend is being abused and stays silent? I hate it, and I'm starting to hate me.

ele

There is a fair in town this week and Brie and Casey should be here any minute to pick me up. We're meeting Ethan and the band there. Brie basically strong-armed me into going so that she could have a legitimate reason to hang around Jackson.

The last time I went to a fair I was thirteen. Dad took Em and I. He loved carnivals and rides; he dared us to go on some insane bungee ball where you're caged in and then catapulted into the air at warp speed. Of course, being the cocky self-assured thirteen-year-olds that we were, there was no way we were backing down. We paid our $5, then sat back and endured the worst fifteen seconds known to mankind. I'd eaten a red popsicle before the ride. Big mistake—I'd lost my stomach almost instantly and it was not pretty. Emily was traumatized by the whole thing and by the time Dad had gotten us all cleaned up and stopped laughing, I vowed I'd never go to a fair again. The memory has me chuckling to myself as we walk up to the entrance and meet the guys. Casey's eying me like I'm some sort of mental case.

"You know, Blair, it's supposed to be the first sign of madness to talk to yourself, but you're a whole nutha level. You just muttered to yourself and then started laughing creepily."

I can't help but break out into a proper laugh then and just stick my tongue out at her.

Ethan, Jackson, TJ, Drew and Dannii are all standing at the entrance paying as we walk up and join them.

Ethan draws me in and kisses me like he hasn't just

seen me at school earlier.

"Dude, get a room!" TJ muses. "You're worse than those two fuckers," he says tilting his head to Drew and Dannii who stand hand in hand.

"Screw you man, you're just jealous coz you're not getting any!" Drew shouts, flipping him the bird.

"I'm getting plenty, asshole, just ask your mom!" Everyone bursts out laughing except for Drew, who looks like he wants to kill TJ, which just makes everyone laugh harder.

We head over to a ride called The Graviton, which is basically a huge barrel with angled padded panels lining the inside walls. The riders lean against them and the whole thing lifts into the air and spins ridiculously fast on a tilt. It removes the floor and the idiots inside are pinned with centrifugal force to the pads. I feel sick just looking at it.

Ethan narrows his gaze at me. "You look freaked out, I don't think you should ride this thing. Maybe you should stand and hold our jackets and we'll go on something a little steadier next."

My mouth falls open and my jaw nearly hits the floor. What a douche!

"No, Mr. Go-on-something-a-bit-steadier, I'll be fine on this thanks."

The corners of his mouth lift as he tries to suppress a smile. "If you're sure, Princess."

"I'm sure," I tell him, faking a confidence that I don't at all feel. In fact I'm practically shitting myself as we board the ride and get into position. I'm trembling so much I think I'm gonna toss my cookies before the stupid ride even starts. Jackson, who's positioned opposite me, looks like he's thinking the same thing.

"Yo Blair, if you're gonna hurl make sure you angle your face away from me," he shouts, and everyone around us spins their head to see whether or not he's joking. I grasp a hold of Ethan's hand and squeeze until my knuckles turn white with the force of it.

"Jeez, Princess, that hurts," Ethan says grinning like a freaking idiot. "Wishing you were standing holding our jackets now, huh?" He's being playful but I want to punch him.

"Oh my god, oh my god, why am I on here?" I start chanting. He leans in and kisses my temple just as the ride begins with no freaking warning and the barrel starts to spin. It's not horrendously fast to begin with but it's quickly picking up pace. The lights from the other rides all flash and blur together making me dizzy as the heavy rock music starts to kick in.

I suddenly have visions of red popsicles and it's threatening to make me chuck as the wind whips my ponytail across my face. The speed picks up and the faster the ride spins, the more panicked I become that I'm about to lose it and throw up. I'm aware Ethan still has a hold of my hand and I'm pretty fucking glad since my feet no longer seem to be touching the ground and my face is being pressed to the side by the force. The ride finally comes to a stop after a few god-awful minutes and everyone's laughing and saying how awesome it was. I'm still pinned to the wall and I'm pretty sure if I try and walk I'm just going to collapse because my legs have turned to Jell-O.

"You look like you really enjoyed that," Ethan says as he pulls on my hand for me to follow him off the ride.

"Don't ever let me get on another thing like this ever," I say, pouting. "I don't think I can feel my legs."

He leans in and presses a quick kiss to the tip of my nose.

"You are pretty adorable when you try to act all tough," he says and before I realize what's happened, he's thrown me on his back and starts walking down the ramp towards the others.

ele

TJ and Jackson have just about OD'd on cotton candy, Drew looks pissed as he carries around a giant pink teddy bear the size of a seven-year-old, that Dannii insisted he won for her, and Brie and Case are walking ahead of us talking a million miles an hour. Ethan nudges me and tilts his chin in the direction of a ride that's called The Grand Canyon.

"Wanna try It?" he asks, swinging our linked hands back and forth. It appears to be a roller coaster made to look like an old mining train.

"Nah, I'm good. You know, the Grand Canyon and Vegas are on Emily's list. We talked about taking a road trip to the canyon before she died," I tell him in a somber voice. "We'd just watched *Thelma and Louise* when she mentioned it, so it kinda put me off." I smile bumping his shoulder.

"Didn't they drive their Thunderbird over the edge at the end?" he asks, eyes wide.

"Yup, hence I didn't jump at the chance to take a trip there after watching a film with my dying best friend about a pair of friends that drive over the edge because they feel like they have nothing left."

"Shit," he breathes out. "So you think she'd have wanted you to drive over the edge with her?" His eyebrows are drawn in, frowning.

I let out a chuckle and smile. "Nah...but I wasn't about to find out."

"How about I take you?" he asks.

"What, to go commit suicide?" I deadpan.

"No, freak!" He laughs. "If it's on her list, let's drive out and camp there. We could go for the weekend, we can drive to Vegas while we're at it and then you can cross it off the list."

"You're serious?"

"Deadly." He laughs again, pulling me to him and kissing my forehead.

"Okay then, you're on." I smile and then wonder how the hell I'm gonna pitch this to my mom.

ele

"Absolutely not," Mom clips out.

"But Moooommm!" I whine. "I'm eighteen, why can't I go camping with my boyfriend?"

"Is that a serious question, Blair? Do you want a list?"

"Um, yeah I kinda do."

"Fine. A. You're too young to go wandering around in the desert by yourselves. B. You'll probably end up murdered, and three, if you're not murdered you'll more than likely come back pregnant." She announces all of this to me like I'm an idiot for asking.

"You mean C."

"What?"

"You mean C. You said A, B, Three. It should have been C."

"Don't be a smart ass, Blair, you're not going." she tells me as she folds the laundry.

"Mom, I'm eighteen, it's a weekend camping. I'm not joining some commune and participating in group sex!" I'm frustrated as hell with her. I get that she worries, I'm her only daughter and she's my mother. But I'm not some silly little girl. Half the time I'm more responsible than she is.

"I know you're not stupid, Blair, but what if something were to happen to you, huh?"

"Like what? It's a few hours' drive, it's not like I'm going overseas." I'm beginning to sound like a petulant child and I need to rein it in.

"Honey, nine hours is not a few. I said no, now let's leave it, please."

"This is bullshit!" I say tossing the shirt I was folding back into the basket and giving her a pointed look. "You go away for work all the time and leave me here alone for as long as a week! I don't see the difference. Anything that I could get up to camping, I could just as easily do right here." I frown, picking the shirt back up and re-folding it. "What's really bothering you, Mom?"

"I just," she pinches the bridge of her nose and exhales. "You're just growing up too fast, is all. You'll be off at college soon and it's just so overwhelming having your baby come and ask if she can go camping alone with a boy in the middle of the desert." She pulls a fabric softener sheet from a pair of pants and folds them without looking up. "It's scary doing all this on your own, not having anyone to back up your decisions."

I sigh and walk around the laundry basket to give her a hug, "I miss Dad, too," I tell her, breathing her in.

"I know you do, honey. I'm sorry, I think I'm just having a bad day." Let's shelve this conversation and we'll talk about it after dinner. Deal?"

"Deal," I tell her, bumping the dryer door shut with my hip; I pick up the basket and carry it up the stairs.

"To be continued then!" I shout out and listen to her laugh in reply.

Ethan

"NOW, *THAT'S* WHAT I'm talking about—that was excellent, Ethan," Steve says slapping my back and causing beads of sweat to slide down my forehead and into my eyes. "You'll nail the entrance exam if you play like that." He smiles.

"That's the plan," I answer as I grab the hem of my shirt and wipe at my face. I've been at the piano three hours solid, my arms and shoulders are aching and I need to go change my shirt.

"Good practice. I'll see you tomorrow, same time!" Steve shouts as I make my way to the guys' locker room down the hall.

"Dude, what's up? You busy now?" Jackson asks barreling through the doors as I'm changing. I pull my shirt over my head and toss it on the bench. I have a beater on under my shirt since I'm still bruised and didn't want anyone to notice. Trouble is, it's fucking boiling. I felt like I was about to pass out in the music room.

"Ain't got any plans, you?"

"Heading back to mine, wanna come play video games?"

"Dude you're so rock and roll."

"Fuck you, asshole!" he says. "You want in or not?"

"Sure," I tell him and pull my phone from my locker. I send a text to Blair telling her I'm going to Jackson's and I'll call her later and toss my cell back into my open locker.

Jackson's watching me with a smug look on his face and his eyebrows raised.

"What?"

"Texting the ball and chain to make sure it's cool to come out and play." He laughs. "Never thought I'd see the day Ethan Jamison was pussy whipped." He's holding his arm out in front of him, doing a stupid whipping motion. I toss my deodorant can at him.

"I'm not whipped, asshole."

"No…so that wasn't Blair you just texted?" He laughs rubbing at the spot on his arm where the canister struck.

"No dickhead," I lie.

"You're a shit liar, E." He smirks and walks out the locker room, still making the whipping noises and I laugh to myself. Truth is, I'm completely whipped and I couldn't give a shit. Hell, I think I even kinda like it.

elle

"You totally suck at this game," Jackson informs me,

throwing his control pad onto the floor in front of him.

"Yeah, that's because I have a life, dude. I don't sit in my basement playing video games every night," I say, shrugging my shoulders.

"I don't just play video games, I read too." He grins, waiting for my response to the out-and-out lie.

I throw my head back in laughter. I'm willing to bet my car that he doesn't own a single book that isn't for school. "Why do I have a hard time believing that, bro?"

He shakes his head and slaps his hand across his chest dramatically in mock disgust. "I'll have you know I have an extensive range of reading materials down here." He reaches under the sofa we're sitting on and pulls out a stack of Playboys. "See?"

I bust out laughing as he pushes them back into their hiding spot.

"You need to get laid, you're turning into a creeper."

"Tell me about it." He sighs and twists so that he's facing me. "So I'm pretty sure that Brie's game for it, ever since you started dating Blair she's moved her attention onto me."

"Yeah, I'd noticed that, thank god," I say, smiling. "The girl's persistent, I'll give her that."

"I'd give her whatever she wanted. Have you not seen her rack?" He pulls a weird pout and pretends to weigh a pair of tits in front of his chest.

"Not her rack I'm interested in."

He groans and falls back against the cushions, "Whipped!"

"Yeah, yeah." I flip him the bird and he picks his controller up again. "Go again?"

"Nah bro, gonna make a move, catch you later," I tell him, standing and patting my pockets down to find my keys.

"Later dude," he calls out, and as I'm leaving the room I hear a loud whipping noise. Asshole.

I'M ABOUT TO climb into my car when my cell beeps; I pull it out and look at the screen, one new message from Blair.

From: Princess
The GC and Vegas is ON!!!
B xxx

I pull up her number and hit dial, it rings twice before she answers in a high-pitched squeal.

"She caved!"

"Hey Princess, that's awesome news," I say around my smile because it *is* awesome. A whole weekend alone together. My dick twitches at the thought of all of the things we could get up to.

"Yup, I kind of forgot to mention that we'd be heading to Vegas too, but she took so much persuading to let me go to the Grand Canyon, I didn't want to push my luck."

"Guess we better decide when to go and organize this thing, then."

"Eeeek I'm so freaking excited!"

I can't control the laugh that bubbles from my chest.

"Babe did you just say 'Eek'?"

"Yeah, whatever get over it, I'm hyper," she tells me

and I can practically hear the smile in her voice.

"You're such a dork, I love it." The words are out before I can stop them and I widen my eyes in surprise at how easily the word love just slipped out of my mouth. It's not a word I'm accustomed to using. I hold my breath waiting for her to reply.

"I'm pretty sure dork isn't a term of endearment…but I'll let it slide 'cause you're hot," she retorts and I exhale letting my shoulders drop.

"You forgot intelligent, charming, witty, charisma—"

"Oh, and not to mention modest…now who's the dork?" She's chuckling to herself and I like that I can make her sound so happy.

"Okay Princess, I'm heading home from Jacksons, I'll see you at school tomorrow?"

"You will, night Ethan." She disconnects the call, and I climb into my car and head home. I can't knock the smile off my face at the thought of this trip. It's not lost on me that it would be the perfect opportunity for us to sleep together; I'm pretty sure that's where things are heading. She's already told me that she's never had a relationship before and I've taken that to mean that she's still a virgin, too. Shit, I hope she is, the thought of another guy anywhere near her makes my blood boil. I can feel my body tense at the thought of her being naked with someone other than me. Even just kissing another guy. I look down to see that I've inadvertently gripped the steering wheel so tight that my knuckles have turned white.

I'm hit with the sudden realization that I've never really had a relationship either, but I've had a shit ton of sex. What if she's not okay with that? I can't change the past.

I've never really given it a thought until now. I know it makes me a total asshole, but it would bother me if the tables were turned. Just the thought makes my stomach coil. I hope she doesn't feel this way about my sexual history. I hand-on-heart wish I'd never screwed around, having meaningless sex with girls that I can't even remember the names of. If I'd known I would meet Blair, feel the things I'm feeling, I'd have never slept with anyone. I'd have waited for her. She's the type of girl that you'd do that for. I've spent the last god knows how long ripping into Drew for the way he acts about Dannii. I never got it before. I do now. Dannii is Drew's game changer, and Blair Thomas is mine.

Chapter 21

Blair

"PRINCESS?" HIS VOICE jolts me back to earth as his kisses move back up from my neck, across my jaw and meet my lips again.

"…Yeah?" I answer, but I'm not really paying attention to his voice, his lips have me in a trance and it's made my head foggy, I can't concentrate on anything other than how good this feels.

He smiles pulling away from my mouth and his dimples appear in full force.

"Lie back," he says. "Lift your ass a little so I can pull these off."

I instinctively do as he says as he hooks his fingers in the belt loop of my shorts and tugs them down my legs slowly, dropping them somewhere on the floor. His gaze follows the path his hand is traveling between my breasts and down my stomach. Getting dangerously closer and closer to the ache he's causing between my legs. I swallow hard as his fingers rub against my clit through the fabric of my panties and I can feel the wetness pooling there.

He lifts his gaze to meet my eyes with his crooked grin. "So wet for me already," he says as he carefully peels my panties down to gain better access.

My shoulders arch and my head tilts back as he blows a slow steady breath across my core. My heart is pounding so fiercely I can hear it drumming in my ears.

"Do you want me inside of you, Princess?" he asks as he traces circles on the inside of my thighs with his fingertips.

"Yes," I gasp out, because at this moment it's the only thing I want. I need him to ease the ache that's building with every second as he tortures my thighs and teases me.

He pushes my knees apart and positions himself—standing—between my legs.

"You have to tell me what you want me to do, Blair."

A wave of pure heat and desire crashes over me as he stands waiting for me to respond. I try to steady my breathing by taking a long calming breath. I'm anything but calm, I'm excited and scared and so freaking turned on that I'm not sure what to do with myself. I whisper the words so softly that I'm not sure if he can even hear me. "I need to feel you inside me."

His eyes are hooded and his gaze so intense I can feel the heat of it. Goose bumps cover my entire body as he leans over me, bringing his face just inches from mine.

Laughter erupts all around me, jolting me awake as I sit up panicked by the outburst. My heart's slamming against my chest and I'm struggling to regain my breath. I look around to get my bearings. I don't recognize my surroundings for a few seconds, when a fresh wave of laughter cuts through the air.

I whip my head around to see Brie and Casey in a fit of hysterics across the bed. My mind suddenly clears and my brain kicks back into gear—I'm at Brie's house, we were watching a movie.

"What the fuck, chuck?" Casey cries out as she's holding her sides and giggling like a hyena.

"Ethan…oh I need to feel you!" Brie says in a breathy maiden voice. I feel a tsunami of mortification crash over me as I realize I was dreaming, and those two had front row seats to the show.

"Shit, was I saying that out loud?" My cheeks feel like they're on fire and I drop my head into my hands, shaking it. "Oh god…" I groan out, as both girls collapse in yet another round of laughter. I'm taking their hysterics as a yes to my question. God. Kill. Me. Now!

Brie's almost hyperventilating with laughter as she clips out, "That was better than the restaurant scene in *When Harry Met Sally*! Gosh, your dreams are vivid, huh?"

I grab a pillow from beside me and toss it at her as hard as I can, but she deflects it and I can't help the bubbles of laughter that erupt from my own chest. I figure it's better to laugh at myself than cry in shame.

"Sounds like you and Ethan are getting your freak on even in your sleep. I heard rumors that the boy's got skills, but damn girl, you looked like you were about to come just dreaming about him."

"Oh my god, Casey shut up!" I squeal, struggling to find my composure.

"Ah, get over it. Everyone has a porno dream at some

point, just not usually while watching a movie with their girlfriends," she manages to say through her laughter.

I can't think of a single moment when I've been this embarrassed. And I do a lot of embarrassing shit.

"So is he as good in bed in real life?" Brie asks, raising her eyebrows and grinning like a Cheshire cat.

"I wouldn't know, we haven't slept together yet."

The room goes deathly silent as both girls' mouths drop open and they gawk at me.

"What?" The staring and silence is making me feel all kinds of awkward.

"Hold on a sec, re-the fuck-wind!" Casey bites out.

"You've been dating Ethan Jamison for over a month and you haven't slept together yet?" Brie asks, her eyes wide as she takes in the 'um…yeah' expression I'm obviously wearing. She shakes her head like it's the most unfathomable concept that's ever been put to her. I stare blankly back as her face scrunches up in confusion. You'd think I'd just asked her to explain the theory behind Quantum Entanglement.

"We've done other stuff," I offer, suddenly feeling conscious of why Ethan and I haven't gone further. I've never been one to bow to peer pressure and I'm not sure now what has me so eager to defend our relationship. It feels like I have this overwhelming compulsion to seek confirmation that what we're doing is normal. That our relationship is as it should be.

"Wow!" Casey breathes out. "He's usually got a girl's panties off before she's even told him her name."

"Um, shut up! Thant's my boyfriend you're talking about"

"Sorry, that sounded way less harsh in my head," she

says with a meek expression. "But you can't deny his rep, Blair. Has he tried to get in your panties yet?"

I feel my cheeks color again but this time my embarrassment is laced with a tinge of anger, both for the fact that Casey even asked that question and that Ethan really hasn't tried very hard.

"Not really. Well, we've fooled around and he's got me off, but we haven't gone any further than that." Why the hell I'm telling them this I have no idea. I'm not the girlie gossip type; in fact, I'm completely the opposite. My private life has always stayed private. The only person I ever shared things like this with was Em, and that's the way I liked it. Apparently now I'm happy to discuss my sex life. Who am I?

"Wow," Casey says.

"Will you stop saying 'wow'? You're making me freak out," I shoot, as Casey holds her hands up in surrender.

"Do you think he doesn't want to sleep with me?" I ask. I can hear the uncertainty in my own voice and it's irritating the shit out of me. I'm not this person; I'm not this weak.

"Blair, relax, trust me…Ethan Jamison wants to sleep with you. It's written all over that sexy face of his every time he sees you. Actually, I kinda hate you," Brie says smiling and I feel my shoulders relax slightly as I exhale and take in what she's said.

"Yup, that boy has got it bad for you. I was just surprised, is all. He's definitely turned over a new leaf with you."

"Thanks, Brie." I smile and although her words have

eased me a little, I can't help the nagging question I still have at the back of my mind: why hasn't he made a move?

I sit back and draw my legs up against my chest and glance over to the television; the movie credits are rolling and I realize that I slept through the whole thing.

Brie reaches across and grabs the remote to stop the movie.

"If I put another one on, do you think you could manage to stay awake and watch it with us without passing out and having more sex dreams?"

I stick my tongue out like a twelve-year-old and laugh.

"Yes, I think I can manage that." I smile as she stands and motions for us to follow as she hurries out of her room.

"Cool, let's go make popcorn first."

"I didn't mean to make you pissed. If I overstepped the mark I'm sorry," Casey says as we follow Brie.

"Nah, it's fine," I tell her. And actually it is. For the first time since Emily died, I feel like I have girlfriends again. The thought is bittersweet.

Chapter 22

Ethan

I'M OUT IN the yard shooting hoops when my mom pulls into the drive. She'd dropped my dad off at the marina; he's going on his annual fishing trip with a few of his buddies from the force and I couldn't be happier. A whole week of not treading on eggshells sounds like nirvana. There's something wrong when a father spending a week away from home is the highlight of his kid's year.

"Hey honey, can you help me with these bags?" Mom shouts from the back of her car.

I sink my last shot and retrieve the basketball, holding it propped against my hip as I walk around the car to help her.

"Go inside, I got this," I say as I move her out of the way and scoop up the three grocery bags in one hand. I step away from the trunk as she closes it and walks inside holding the door for me.

"Thank you," she says as I deposit the bags onto the

kitchen island. I start riffling through them until I find the package of Tastykakes.

"Don't eat them ye—" Mom shouts as I push a whole one into my mouth.

"What?" I ask around a mouthful of cake and she shakes her head.

"I'm about to make dinner—don't eat anymore," she warns and turns to start putting the groceries away,

I slip another cake out of the packet and stuff it into my mouth thinking I've gotten away with it. She has her head in the refrigerator and calls out to me without even turning around.

"Do you think I'm stupid Ethan? Stop shoveling down cakes."

What is it about moms? Do they have an invisible third eye in the back of their heads or something?

"I'm not," I reply.

She straightens and turns to look at me. "You're a terrible liar Ethan." She says tutting her disapproval and I roll my eyes.

It's funny how backward she seems to have her priorities. She'll speak up to stop me from ruining my dinner, but not to save me from a beating. I don't remember our relationship always feeling this strained. I guess over time and the more frequently Dad lashes out, the more I resent her. It's no wonder I don't like spending time at home, I'm not the least bit comfortable here and she must sense it. We've fallen into the trap of make believing we're a normal family when Dad's not on the scene. But it's fake, and we both know it.

"Go wash up for dinner. It won't take long." Her voice is laced with an emotion I can't quite put my finger on. Worry, maybe.

"Yes, ma'am," I answer and head upstairs to take a quick shower. I need to let the hot water soak my aching shoulders. I've spent hours at the piano and then on my guitar today. I only went outside to shoot hoops so I could get some fresh air.

It takes me less than ten minutes under the hot spray to feel better. I climb out of the shower and head back into my room to grab a fresh pair of underwear. I dress quickly in an old pair of jeans and a faded Stones t-shirt that I've had forever.

I make my way down to the kitchen and Mom's sitting at the table waiting on me. I take my seat across from her and she gives me a weak smile.

"How's your day been?" she asks. It's one of those questions she's not really concerned about the answer to. I could probably tell her that I hung out with a bunch of gangsters and robbed the convenience store and she'd nod her head and say, 'that's nice, dear'.

"Okay, yours?" I reply instead.

"Getting better." She takes the serving spoons and deposits a huge mass of spaghetti onto my plate.

"I was wanting to have a talk to—" my cell ringing cuts her off. I stand up to get it out from my back pocket and she shoots me the glare. "No cell phones at the dinner table, Ethan. You know the rules."

I look down at the screen and notice it's Blair's name flashing.

"Chill, Mom, he's not here," I say as I sit back down and answer the call.

Mom throws her arms up in defeat and then busies

herself fixing a plate of her own.

"Hey babe, what you up to?" Blair's cheery voice echoes in my ear.

"Just about to have dinner, you?"

"I'm starving! My mom's not home from work yet so I was waiting to eat with her, but she just texted that she was working late on some account. Anyway, enough about that. I wanted to know if we could get together and plan this trip?" She sounds like an overexcited kid on Christmas Eve.

"Come over here, I'll feed you and then we can make plans?" I ask, looking at my mom for confirmation. She leans back in her chair and drops her fork onto her plate dramatically. I'm guessing she's not happy with my invite, but it's done now so she'll have to get over it.

"Okay, if you're sure, I'll come now."

"Okay Princess, see you in a few." I end the call tossing my cell onto the table.

"Hope you don't mind," I offer as Mom sits forward again and sighs before answering.

"No honey, that's fine." The words coming out of her mouth don't match the mood she looks to be in.

"Anyway, you were saying something before she called?" I tilt my chin waiting for her to continue.

"Nothing important," she says around a sip of her wine. "Let me cover this food and we'll all eat together when Blair gets here."

"Okay…Mom is everything alright?" She looks tired and worn out, her dark hair is devoid of any shine, and her skin looks pasty and pale. She's a beautiful woman, don't get me wrong. I have to put up with a shit ton of comments about her from the guys, but today she's really not looking her best. She's tiny anyway, but today she seems to look even smaller.

"I'm good, Ethan, don't be worrying about me." She plasters a fake smile across her face that doesn't meet her eyes, but if that's the way she wants to play it I'll go along.

"So you and Blair must be getting serious?" she asks, taking another sip of her drink.

"Could say that." I'm not quite sure what other answer to give her.

"So…tell me about her then. I don't know anything about the girl that's captured my son's heart."

I almost choke on my water and lift my eyes to meet hers. I think about the question and realize that even though we've been dating a while now I don't actually know much about her that would make for suitable dinner conversation. I need to fix that; it's awkward when someone asks you about your girlfriend and all you can give them is her name and the fact that she doesn't like meatball pizza and has eclectic taste in music.

"What do you want to know?"

"I don't know—where did you guys meet? What are her parents like? Anything?"

I inwardly smile; at least I can answer these.

"She's my math tutor," I grin and continue, "that's how we met. As for her parents, she lives with her mom, Susan. She's nice. I've only met her a couple of times. Her dad died a few years back of a heart attack and as far as I'm aware, there's no stepdad or potential stepdad in the picture."

Mom smiles and nods, contemplating my answers.

The doorbell breaks the silence and I jog over to go

let her in.

"Hey you," I say, bending and placing a soft kiss on her forehead. She always smells of strawberries.

"Are you sniffing my hair, creeper?"

I laugh and step aside, taking her jacket.

"You shouldn't smell so good," I say tapping her ass and she jolts forward in surprise. "We were just talking about you."

Her eyes widen and she stops walking. "All good, I hope?"

"Of course. Now come on into the kitchen and let me feed you."

She brings her hand above her eye in a mock salute and bumps her arm against mine.

"Dork"

"Whatever, creeper," she chuckles as we head to the kitchen.

"Blair honey, how are you?" my mom says, enveloping her in a hug then pushing her back and holding onto her arms as if inspecting her. I kind of feel bad for her. I know she'll be feeling awkward as hell. My mom's definitely the touchy-feely type.

"I'm great, thank you Mrs. Jami-oh, I mean Moira. Thank you for having me over. I realize I've kind of hijacked your dinner. You really didn't have to feed me tonight."

"Hush your mouth, you can come any time you like. It's only pasta; I hope that's okay?" she says while directing Blair around the table to take a seat. I hope she's prepared herself for the billion questions my mom's gonna unleash on her ass. Her sweet little ass...man, I'm a pervert.

ele

"Okay, so your mom's kind of intense," she tells me as she's lounging on my bed, propped up on her elbows and tapping away at the keyboard on my laptop.

"Yeah, sorry about the twenty questions. She's doesn't get out much." I look over my shoulder as I rifle through the papers on my desk.

"What are you looking for?"

"I printed out some places we could visit. I can't find them, though. I put them on here, I'm sure of it." I tell her, still leafing through all the crap.

"Relax, I'll just check your history," she says, and like a fucking moron I agree. It takes my brain a couple of seconds to catch up with my mouth before I realize that I've just given her the green light to go through my Internet history. FUCK!

She raises her head above the laptop screen and narrows her eyes at me. "Baby?"

Oh my fucking god she's seen it. "Yeah?" I'm trying for nonchalance but failing miserably.

"Um…why are you searching Google for tips to avoid premature ejaculation?" I can tell that she's trying her damnedest not to laugh but the corners of her mouth are twitching and she's biting her bottom lip so hard it's going white from the pressure.

I'd searched it the other night after almost losing it while we were making out. This girl does something to me and I swear it's not normal. I'm an eighteen-year-old not a thirteen-year-old, but apparently my raging hormones haven't gotten the memo.

I'm not okay with lying to her but on this occasion I'll let it slide, "What? No way, let me see?"

She raises her eyebrows and smirks, spinning the laptop around. I look at the history for a second, willing myself to come up with a half decent explanation. "Ah, look." I point at the screen. "Must have been Jackson, he was here yesterday and borrowed the laptop." I'm feeling pretty smug that I've come up with an excuse.

"Jackson came here, borrowed your laptop, and then searched about premature ejaculation?" She knows I'm full of shit but I started this and now I kind of feel like I need to run with it.

"Yup."

She busts out laughing and rolls onto her side. "Why the hell would he even do that?"

"Um…he has a little sister, I'm guessing the computers at their house have like a child protection thing on them so they can't search anything adult." I'm pretty fucking impressed at how quickly that came out.

"Makes sense, I guess. Better warn Brie that her target has trouble downstairs." She's chuckling away to herself while I stand over her, my heart racing, my palms sweating from clenching my fists so hard.

Note to self: always delete search history.

Chapter 23

Blair

I'M ALMOST WETTING myself at the lies he's trying to sell me. There is no way on this planet that he didn't perform that search himself. It's cute how panicked he looked when I questioned it.

"Scoot over," he tells me, positioning himself next to me so he can see the computer.

"So, are we gonna plan this trip, or what? I kinda just thought we'd jump in my car and drive to the Canyon, set up camp and that would be that."

I smile at how simple he makes it sound. "First off, I'm not sure you can just set up camp anywhere in the desert. What about snakes and mountain lions?"

"Snakes?" His eyes widen and bore into mine.

"Aw, Ethan, are you scared of snakes?" I say in my best baby voice.

He straightens his shoulders in defiance. "Course I'm not scared, just didn't cross my mind that there'd be snakes, is all."

"Uh-huh, not scared my ass."

His eyes trail over me and I instantly feel my heart rate kick up a notch.

"You do have a fine ass, Princess," he tells me, squeezing it, sending a jolt of electricity racing through my skin. I shiver and he makes a low growling noise as he moves in and claims my mouth. His kiss is hot and urgent, making all the tiny little hairs on the back of my neck stand on end. His hands slide into my hair as he teases me with his tongue.

"Do you want to sleep with me, Ethan?" I breathe against his lips and he stills, his eyes widening.

"Shit no, I don't mean now. I meant like…in general?" I stammer out as he's looking at me blankly. "It's just, well, you haven't really tried…and well, you have a rep for getting into a girl's pants before you get her name…we've been dating for—" He puts his hand up silencing me from my nervous rant and I can feel the heat spread across my cheeks, I'm all kinds of embarrassed.

"What's brought this on?" He's smiling but there's something else behind that smile. He's wearing an expression that I've not noticed before, like I'm the most precious thing in his world. It looks a lot like it could be love. Instead of freaking me out, it has the opposite effect. The thought that this boy may actually love me makes my heart swell inside my chest. I have the sensation of a giant swarm of butterflies taking flight in my stomach.

He's looking at me from under his long dark lashes, his clear blue eyes are heavy with desire and he's wearing the crooked grin that makes his dimples pop. I concentrate on the image in front of me, trying to commit it to memory, his beautiful face and messy hair sticking out in all angles. It just about melts me.

"Brie just pointed out that—"

"Whoa, whoa, whoa! Princess, don't ever start a sentence with 'Brie just.'" He grins and I feel my body relax as he raises his hand and runs the back of his fingers down the side of my face.

"Blair, I want to sleep with you, trust me. I really, really want to sleep with you. But I'm not going to rush this. I want to make sure that it's perfect for you."

I'm pretty sure I'm a puddle, slowly dissolving on his bed. I have no idea how to reply to that, so instead I lean forward and press my lips lightly against his. I have to resist the urge to pinch him to make sure that he's real, or maybe pinch myself, to make sure I'm not dreaming again.

I push up so I'm resting on one arm and use the other to slide around his waist, pulling us both closer together. I want tell him that I'm ready now, that no matter what, as long as it's with him, it will be perfect. I don't just want to blurt it out though. I'd attempt to be sexy but in all honesty that's never going to happen. It would be beyond awkward. I think I must have been absent the day they were giving out lessons in sex appeal and flirting. I decide that the direct approach works best for me. Even if it is about as seductive as a wet fish.

"What if I were to tell you that I'm ready now?"

He arches his brow and gives me a pointed look. "I'd say that's pretty fucking mean, since you know my mom's downstairs."

I slap at his arm and laugh. "No asshole, I didn't mean right this second."

"Aw, calling me asshole…you have such sweet pil-low talk, Princess."

"You're a dick, Ethan Jamison!"

"Yeah, I am baby, a huge dick." He puts emphasis on the word huge and wiggles his brows at me. I can't really call him out on that since I've seen him buck naked in freezing cold water, and he still looked pretty huge to me. The thought sends a tingle racing down my spine that makes me shudder.

"You fantasizing about my goods?"

"No!" I answer way too quickly. I may as well have a big red sign across my forehead that reads: LIAR. "Okay, yeah I was, I admit it."

He lunges forward and starts ticking my sides and I squeal twisting and contorting trying to get away. He pins me to the bed sitting over my chest.

"Get off me! I can't breathe!" I shout out between bouts of laughter.

"Nuh-uh, not until you say 'Ethan Jamison is the sex-iest man I have ever laid my pervy little eyes on.'"

"What are we, twelve? Get your butt off of me, I'm a tiny little woman!"

He seems to think that this is hilarious and tickles me more.

"Okay, okay, quit it!" I try twisting away from his at-tack but he's relentless. "Fine, you win! You're the sexiest man I have ever laid my eyes on," I bark out through the laughter.

He stops tickling and rolls off me onto his side. "That wasn't word perfect but I'll let you off."

"I hate being tickled!"

"Really? 'Cause from where I was sitting you looked

to be having fun."

I stick my tongue out at him, blowing a raspberry.

"You're a dork."

"You're an asshole."

"You're kind of perfect."

And there he goes again, killing me with his surprise sweetness. I let out a sigh. "You're forgiven."

"Good, now come over here and kiss me."

So that's what I do. I pour every last bit of emotion I'm feeling in this moment into the kiss, losing myself in the sensation of his tongue moving against mine. His hand is squeezing my waist and all I can hear is the sound of my heart echoing in my ears. He may have just called me perfect but he got it wrong. He's the perfect one.

Chapter 24

Ethan

MOM LEFT A note this morning telling me that there's lasagna in the refrigerator for dinner, and that she has plans after work and won't be back tonight. Dad's still away for the next three nights and my dick is screaming at me, 'tonight's the night!' A few months ago if I'd found myself in this position, the party announcement would already have been texted. Now, I have to figure out the best way to play this. Do I ask Blair over and do the whole romantic night in crap, or do I take her out and then bring her back? I know I'm getting ahead of myself but I haven't gotten laid in almost two months; I don't think I've jerked off this much since I hit thirteen and watched the free ten-minute preview on the adult channel at midnight.

Now that I know Blair wants to take the next step with me, it's like I've been walking around with a permanent hard on. This shit's not funny anymore; my balls have gone beyond blue and are entering into a state of shock.

I scoop up my keys and bag and decide to head to school and tell Blair I have the house to myself. I'll let her call the shots, but shit am I praying that she's gonna want to spend the night. Even if you take sex out of the equation, the thought of going to sleep with her in my bed and waking up to her in the morning, makes me wanna break out into the running man. Who am I kidding—take sex with her out of the equation and I may just fucking cry.

ele

I make it to school in record time, which is pretty scary considering I don't actually remember the drive here. I was too caught up in my fantasy of what could happen tonight when I look up and notice Corey talking to Blair at her locker. He's leaning into her, his body way too close to hers, and she's laughing at something he's saying. I feel like someone's just thrown a bucket of ice water over my good mood.

That pussy better back the hell away from my girl before I lose my shit. I quicken my pace towards them and I'm just a couple of strides away when Corey leans in and kisses Blair on the cheek. What the actual fuck? My stomach hits the floor as she smiles at him and then I'm overcome by a wave of anger so powerful my whole body feels like it's vibrating.

I close the distance in a nanosecond, rage cursing through my veins like white-hot lava. On instinct, I grab Corey by the shirt, pushing him hard into the locker and see his eyes flare before he pushes my chest back from his.

"What the fuck, bro?" he yells in surprise.

"What makes you think you can kiss my fucking girl?" I snarl at him, my fingers biting into my palms, my fists clenched tightly. I'm using every ounce of willpower I have not punch him in the face.

"Chill the hell out, dickhead! We weren't doing anything wrong!" He pushes out of my way and smoothes his shirt down. He looks over to Blair. "I'll see you later," he tells her as he walks away from us, and I instantly want to kill him.

"What the hell was that?" she bites out in a hushed tone, placing books in her locker.

"You tell me?" I almost laugh out. "Why the fuck was he kissing you? And more to the point, why the fuck were you letting him?"

She spins to face me, her eyes narrowed to slits. "It was a kiss on the cheek, you're making out like you caught us rounding third base!"

"How the hell do I know that you haven't? I walk in and you're snuggled up next to that jack hole smiling up at him and letting him kiss you! Don't play me for a fucking fool Blair, what's going on?"

"You're an asshole," she says, shaking her head as she shoulder-barges past me and walks away.

I jog up beside her as she opens the door to her class and pull on her arm. "Wait."

"Let me go, everyone's staring," she hisses. I look into the classroom and sure enough, everyone's eyes are trained on us.

"I don't care, we're not done talking."

She pulls her arm from my grip and leans in close. "You're embarrassing me, we are definitely done talking. Now leave me alone."

With that, she turns and walks into the class, heading to the front and taking a seat without looking back. I feel my skin prickle and not in a good way. My stomach is knotted and I feel like I'm about to lose my breakfast. I want to scream out in frustration and pound my fist into the classroom door. People are still looking from me to her, waiting to see my reaction. I'm not in the mood to put on a fucking show so I pull the strap of my backpack tighter, spin on my heel and make my way to my fist period class. Corey's in that class, and if Blair won't give me any answers, I'll make that prick do it.

ele

I storm into biology class, sending death glares back to where Corey's sitting between Drew and Toby Price. Toby's an absolute monster of a guy; I'm talking seriously huge. A cool guy, though. Been hit one too many times in the head with a football, but I suppose being the star quarterback, you kind of expect it.

"Ah, Mr. Jamison, nice of you to join us. Take a seat quickly please, you're late," Ms. Beckett calls as she's looking up from the textbook she's holding.

I take my seat and crack my neck; I'm coiled like a freaking spring I'm so pissed. How the hell did this morning turn to shit this quickly?

Jackson's eyes are narrowed at me as he silently mouths, "What?"

I shake my head signaling that I really don't wanna talk about it now, then sit for the next hour picturing Blair and Corey screwing behind my back and laughing at me.

163

The sound of the bell and chairs scraping as students busy themselves getting their shit together break up my thoughts. I stay seated and throw my arm out blocking the aisle as Corey attempts to leave.

"I need to speak to you," I tell him, trying to keep my temper at bay. Jackson and Drew look at each other then back to Corey and me.

"What's going on, guys?" Drew asks.

"That's what I want to know." My eyes never leave Corey's.

"I don't know what your problem is man. We were talking, that's it."

"What the fuck were you saying that required you to kiss my girlfriend, then, huh?"

He squares his shoulders and watches as I stand up.

"I didn't know we had an English test today. Blair offered to lend me her notes since I'm in the same class; I kissed her on the cheek and told her she was a lifesaver, is all. Jesus, stop being such a jealous prick, dude."

I instantly feel like a complete tool. I look over to the guys watching the exchange waiting for my reaction.

"Yeah?" I say shrugging my shoulders into my jacket. "Just don't go kissing my girl again and we won't have a problem."

"Whatever dude, you need to relax. That girl's yours and everyone knows it. No need to get your panties in a fucking bunch," he says, smirking at me. "We cool?"

"Yeah dude, we're cool," I say with a fist bump.

"Now I just need to go find Blair and make sure that she's not ready to go slash my tires."

A whipping sound is made from behind me and I turn to see Jackson grinning at me like the moron he is. Drew coughs and whisper shouts, 'whipped', his grin matching Jackson's.

"Assholes, the pair of you!" I laugh as we all make our way out of the classroom.

ℓℓℯ

I've sent three messages saying 'sorry' and it's only lunchtime. She hasn't replied and it's driving me crazy. I hate knowing I've upset her and she's mad at me. This is definitely not how I pictured today going this morning. Everything's turned to shit and the only person to blame is me. I'm standing at her locker waiting for her like a lost fucking puppy feeling sorry for myself. Maybe my dad's onto something; maybe I am just a screw up. I kick at the floor with the toe of my boots, watching as the rubber leaves a mark on the polished floors.

"Excuse me."

My head snaps up and Blair is standing in front of me staring.

"I need to get into my locker, Ethan. Can you please move?" She still sounds pissed and I want to kick my own ass for putting her in that mood.

I step aside slightly as she opens the locker and tosses her bag inside before closing it again.

"I'm sorry."

"So you've said," she replies, rolling her eyes at me.

"Yeah well, I meant it, Princess. I shouldn't have re-acted the way I did. I saw another guy kissing my girl-friend and I didn't like it." I reach out to take her hand but she moves out of my reach.

"You know your reaction was beyond ridiculous, right? And FYI, there are now rumors going around that I'm cheating on you with Corey. I've already heard one girl in the bathroom telling her friend that I'm a whore. Apparently I'm trying to make my way through Kickstart and the volleyball team all before graduation. So you know what? Sorry doesn't really cut it, Ethan."

Okay, so pissed was an understatement. She looks ready to rip my balls off and feed them to me. It takes me a second to register that's she's storming away and all I can do is stand and watch, not knowing what to do. I'm a stupid jealous prick and now she's suffering for it. Dad was right—I'm a total waste of space.

Blair

I'M STORMING TOWARDS the cafeteria, my fists balled and adrenaline coursing through my system, my heart beating painfully against my chest. I'm so freaking mad at Ethan I could scream. I'm willing myself not to look behind to see if he's following me. The angry part of me is praying that he's not and yet the lovesick moron part is kind of hoping that he is. I'm an idiot.

I round the corner to the cafeteria and see Della Fields walking towards me, so I detour and quickly rush into the girls' bathroom. I really hope she didn't notice me; I'm in no mood to take any of her shit today. I quickly walk to one of the stalls and close myself in. I lower the lid on the toilet seat and sit down with my head in my hands when I hear the bathroom door open and a group of girls talking animatedly and giggling. I can easily pick out Della's sugar sweet voice and I sigh. I'm so over this day already.

They're in the middle of some conversation about

how 'totally off the charts hot Sarah Smith's brother is' when I hear my name mentioned and my interest in their airhead rambling is piqued.

"So, she's totally sleeping with Corey behind Ethan's back. She's such a little tramp," one of the girls chimes. I feel my hackles rise and force myself to listen as whoever it is continues. "What the hell does he even see in her, anyway? She's such a freak. Who wears a t-shirt that says 'read books not shirts'? I mean, what the hell does that even mean? That's not funny."

I suppress my laugh and carry on listening to this bitch hate on me for another thirty seconds before a voice that I do recognize joins in. It's Dannii.

"He'll drop her ass soon enough; there's no way he'll let her cheat on him and just sit back and take it. She's strung him along with the good girl act long enough. Ethan's a player—he's ruled by the head in his trousers, not the one on his shoulders. He's probably lining up the revenge fuck as we speak. In fact, I may have to give him a push in the right direction."

"Yeah, my direction," Della replies.

I'm stunned into silence. I thought Dannii was my friend. Yeah, I know we're not close, but she's always acted cool around me. I swallow the bile that's rising in my throat and listen as the voices fade and the bathroom door opens and shuts.

I make my way out of the cubicle and over to the basin to splash some water on my face. I'm more confused than upset by what I've just heard. I look at myself in the mirror for a second. I take in my appearance, my glasses, my shirt and then I think FUCK THEM! I like how I look; I'm not another hooker Barbie clone like they are. I'm a good person. They can hate all they want. I straighten my shoulders and dry off my face with a paper towel, trying to process what to do with what I just heard.

The hall is bustling with students, and as I step out into the flow heading for lunch, my hand is grabbed and I'm pulled through the doorway of an empty classroom.

"Jesus, you scared the shit outta me!" I splutter trying to regain my composure.

"Princess, please forgive me. I acted like a dick this morning but it's only because I'm crazy about you," Ethan says, pulling me close and resting his forehead against mine. "I know Corey was only kissing your cheek as a thank you for the notes. I don't know who started the rumors, but trust me I'll finish them. Blair, please don't be mad at me anymore."

He's pouting and it's too gorgeous to ignore, I want to be mad at him but I can't see it lasting when he's pulling the puppy dog eyes at me; they melt me.

I kiss him briefly and pull back looking at his victorious smile.

"I would never cheat on you, you know that, right?"

"I know, Princess, I just got caught off guard and acted before thinking."

"Yeah well, maybe next time just try and put a little faith in me."

"I'll put whatever you want in you," he says and then winks, flashing me a brilliant white smile and those freaking dimples.

"Perv!"

"Shut up, you know you love it," he tells me as he kisses my forehead.

"Yeah, I kind of do."

ele

We are sitting at the lunch table, Ethan on the bench and me on his knee. I hate sitting in here but I want to send a message to Della and her wolf pack. I'm pretty sure it's working since she couldn't school the scowl on her face when she noticed Ethan and me.

Drew and Dannii walk over to take a seat and Dannii's eyes widen for a second as she takes in my seating arrangement.

"Hey Blair, how are you holding up? I've heard a few rumors this morning, honestly the girls in this school can be such bitches."

"Tell me about it. So far today I've heard three different variations of how much of a cheating slut I am," I say nonchalantly.

I feel Ethan's body tense under mine as he cranes his neck back to look me in the eye.

"People are calling you a slut?"

"Yup," I tell him.

His eyes squeeze shut and he takes a deep breath. "This is bullshit."

"Chill Ethan, she's a big girl. Aren't you Blair?" Dannii says, taking a seat across from us. "You just need to pull on your big girl panties and ignore it." She smiles.

"Nah…I am a slut, they're kind of right, I'm not even wearing panties."

Ethan chokes as TJ busts out laughing and holds out a first for him to bump. Ethan shakes his head glaring at him and Jackson's just about wetting himself at the exchange. Dannii's eyes are wide as she processes what I just said. I smile a huge fake ass grin at her and she returns an equally fake smile back. She's not aware of the fact that I just overheard her little conversation in the bathroom, and that's the way I'm gonna keep it until I can figure out what it is that she's up to.

I feel Ethan's breath race across my neck as he moves his mouth to my ear. "Are you really not wearing panties?" he whispers and I snort laugh as I whip my head around to look at his face.

"It was a joke, you dirty boy," I tease and his fingers pinch my side, making me jump.

"That's a cruel joke," he says, narrowing his eyes at me in mock disappointment. "Do you have plans tonight?" he asks in a hushed voice.

"No…why are we whispering?"

"Because I don't want people to overhear that I have the house to myself tonight."

"PARTY AT ETHAN'S TONIGHT!" TJ announces to the cafeteria in a shout and half the room cheers.

He glares at TJ like he wants to kill him and TJ winks back at him making me chuckle.

"You're a dick, Connors!" Ethan shouts over the noise of people already making plans to carpool and organize kegs.

TJ shrugs his shoulders and smirks, "What time should we come?"

Ethan ignores him and turns his attention back to me.

"You think you could stop over at my house tonight?" His face is so hopeful it's delectable. A wave of excitement and anticipation slides over my body; I tense and clap my hands like an over eager seven-year-old on Christmas morning.

"I'm sure it can be arranged."

He squeezes my waist and plants a quick kiss against my lips. My crappy day is finally looking up.

Chapter 26

Ethan

"HOLY SHIT DUDE, why's there a doll in your bathroom?" TJ emerges from taking a piss and is looking at me like I'm some sort of freak.

"What are you talking about asshole?"

"The ugly ass Barbie sitting on top of your toilet with a knitted fucking dress!"

I laugh realizing what he means. "The dress is hiding the toilet paper, dude."

"Why?"

I think for a second and draw a blank. "Um…I have no idea, actually." It's one of Mom's weird things. Personally, I'd rather look at a roll of toilet paper sitting there than a creepy action figure in a dress that stares at you while you piss.

"I'd hide it if I were you before the guys get here; they see that you have dolls and they'll rip you a new one."

"This is all your fault fucktard, I didn't even want a party. You completely screwed me over, bro."

"Quit whining like a little bitch. It's one night. You're happy to invite the whole goddamn school when I have a party."

He's got me there; his parties are always pretty full-on. "Yeah, but that's at your house, not mine."

"Karma's a bitch, E my man," he says slapping my shoulders. I look around and decide that there's no fucking way I'll get away with having a party in here without someone trashing something.

"Dude, help carry the drinks through to the pool house. We can set up in there, then I'm locking the house. It's outta bounds. My parents will flip if anything gets trashed in here."

"Your call, bro, lead the way," he says picking up the solo cups and bags of ice. This day has been nothing like I imagined after reading Mom's note this morning.

My phone beeps on the counter; I look down at the text from Blair telling me she'll be over in a half hour with the girls. I'm guessing that she means Brie and Casey since I don't think I've ever seen her hang around with anyone other than those two. I can't wait to get this stupid party over and done with so I can spend time with just Blair. My jeans get tight at the thought and I suppress a groan. I look down at my watch and figure it's only a few more hours; it's not going to kill me.

ele

It's killing me! Brie, Casey and Blair just arrived and my jaw is actually aching from how hard it just hit the fucking floor. She looks, just wow. My cock springs to life from across the room at the sight of her. She's wearing a tight green dress that looks like a tank top, only a little longer. It's clinging to her like a second skin and shows off her perfect little body and creamy toned legs. Her long hair's wavy and loose and she's not wearing her glasses. She looks like a super hot sexed-up version of my already sexy girlfriend. I want to shout for everyone to stop what they're doing and get the hell out my house. Party's over. My girl just walked in looking like sex on legs and I need to get in her before I fucking die.

I drag my eyes away from her when I feel my hands getting wet. What the fuck? I've poured my drink all over myself like a complete loser.

Toby and another guy from the football team walk past and stop.

"Fuck me, who's that?" Douchebag says to Toby as he's eye-humping the shit out of my girlfriend.

"Fresh meat," he replies and I almost throw a punch, only almost though. The guy is the size of a house.

"Dude, that fresh meat is my girlfriend. There's plenty of other girls with no morals here, take your pick," I say, smiling. "Oh, and tell your boy there that if he looks at her again like that, he's gonna wish he wore his cup." I put my drink down and make my way over to her. She's scanning the room.

"There you are, how come everyone's out here?" she says making a circling gesture to the pool house.

"I didn't want anything getting trashed in the house, but I don't really care about that at the moment, get over here."

She bites her bottom lip as I take her hand and pull her into me. "You look…" I trail off and place her hand over the tent in my jeans that she's responsible for and her eyes widen as she chuckles.

"Um, babe why are your pants wet?" She looks down smiling and then her eyes return to mine. "That info on Google not do the trick?"

It takes me a second to realize what she means and me eyes almost bug out of my head.

"What? Wait, no. I mean…not no it didn't work… shit, baby it's just water I spilled."

She throws her head back and clutches her side laughing at me, actually laughing!

"Uh-huh, I believe you," she manages to get out through the chuckles and although I'm totally mortified that she thinks I just shot my load in my pants, I can't help but laugh at how much she's laughing. Then it hits me like a sledgehammer straight to the chest, knocking all the air from lungs. It leaves my heart raw and exposed. I'm not just crazy about this girl, I passed crazy a long time ago. Maybe it was today when I saw Corey kiss her, maybe it was when we spoke after she walked in on my dad and me, or maybe it was the second she called me out for staring at her chest in the library that I knew this girl would change everything. I'm not just crazy about her—I love her.

ele

I finally manage to get the last few guys to leave; it's just passed midnight so I'm pretty impressed with myself. Apart from one girl puking all over Mom's flowerbed I think it's gone well. The guys and I played a few songs, which can count as our practice session because there's no way I'm going to get up early in the morning and go over to Jackson's if Blair is in my bed.

I walk back into the pool house with another trash sack to get rid of the few remaining discarded solo cups and smile down at Blair who fell asleep just after everyone started to leave. I'm happy it's not because of alcohol; she told me that she's still off liquor since TJ's party. I can't say that I blame her; she doesn't do things half-ass so it's best if she doesn't drink.

I finish tidying the pool house listening to the tiny little snores and mumbles she's making and it's cute as hell. I don't know if this makes me a creeper or not, but I pull my cell out and take a picture of her sleeping. She's too fucking perfect not to. The sound of the flash disturbs her and her eyes flutter a few times before she rubs at them and then sits up.

"What time is it?" she asks, her voice thick with sleep.

"A little after midnight, Princess. You wanna come into the house and spend the night still?" I'm holding my breath praying that she hasn't changed her mind but I don't want her to feel like she has to stay. "I can drive you home, if you've changed your mind."

She wipes her eyes again and then yawns, stretching her arms above her head and arching her back.

"The only place I want to go, Ethan, is to your room."

I mentally give myself a high-five and smile down at her sleepy form. I lean across and scoop her up against my chest and her eyes widen for a second before she relaxes.

"You don't have to carry me, you know, my legs work just fine."

"I wanna carry you. Plus, you're not wearing any shoes. I haven't seen them anywhere so let me carry you."

Okay so that's a lie; I put her shoes away when I was tidying. I just wanted a reason to hold her without her thinking I was a complete pansy-ass. I make my way across the yard and through to the kitchen. I sit her on the island and position myself between her legs.

"Let me quickly lock up and then we can go to bed."

"Hmmm," she practically purrs as I lean in and kiss the side of her neck.

"Feels so nice, Ethan."

I force myself to pull away and make sure everything is secure, asking if she wants anything to eat or drink before we head upstairs. She shakes her head and hops off the island.

"Lead the way, sexy," she tells me, pinching my ass. My dick is so hard right now I'm almost positive if she touches it the thing will just blow. I need to calm the fuck down and remind myself I'm not a horny thirteen-year-old anymore.

"Follow me," I tell her shooting her what I assume is a pretty huge shit-eating grin as I take her hand and lead her through the hall.

"Wait!" She stops in her tracks, motioning to the dining room and points over to the piano. "We've been dating for ages and I still haven't heard my so-called musical genius boyfriend play the piano."

I smile and lead her into the room and sit her on the side of the bench with me as I flex my fingers out in-font of me.

"Any requests?"

Her smile is huge. "Anything pretty."

I begin to play *All of Me* by John Legend and she watches me wide-eyed as the music fills the empty room. I close my eyes and sing the words softly, getting lost in the moment. I enjoy playing the guitar and being part of the band, it's fun and I'm good at it. But I love this; playing the piano has always been my way of expressing myself without having to use words. I feel freer when I'm playing. I bring the piece to its end and turn to look at Blair.

"Wow!" she sighs and leans forward, resting her forehead against mine. "That was beautiful. I had no idea you could play like that. I know you're supposed to be going to some fancy music school, but that was just … beautiful."

I laugh quietly and tilt my head so I can kiss her lips.

"I think you should take me upstairs now," she whispers.

I pull her up from the bench; she certainly doesn't need to ask twice.

Chapter 27

Blair

ETHAN LEADS ME by the hand upstairs to his room. My whole body is vibrating with the tingling sensations his touch elicits. I'm thrumming with nervous anticipation, my stomach is knotted and I'm more than a little anxious. I know that I'm about to lose my virginity and as much as I want to, I'm scared of how inexperienced I am, and how Ethan is anything but. I want him more than I've ever wanted anything. I'm ready for this to happen, but I can't deny that the situation has me literally trembling now that it's real. I'm wondering if this will change me, make me feel any different, see things from a new perspective. What if it's too painful or just really bad? What if it's amazing and I turn into some sex-crazed hussy? I feel like I'm standing at the edge of a cliff ready to jump and when I do everything will change.

We walk silently into Ethan's room and my overnight bag is sitting at the end of his bed.

"I brought your things up here earlier. You can take a shower or freshen up — whatever, in my bathroom." He points to the door in the corner of the room. "I'm gonna take a quick shower across the hall. You should find everything you need, there are fresh towels already in there."

"Okay baby, thank you, I won't take long." I scoop my bag up from his bed and make my way into the bathroom.

I stare at my reflection in the mirror and will myself to relax while brushing my teeth. Come on, Blair, you want this. Pull yourself together.

I square my shoulders and take a long deep breath, then strip down and climb into the shower, enjoying the spray against my back. I go to pick up my body wash and realize that I didn't bring it in here with me; I look around the shower cubicle taking in all of Ethan's toiletries.

I choose a bottle that looks the most feminine and squirt a little of the liquid into my hand and bring it up-to my face to smell. The last thing I want is to climb into bed with him smelling like a man. I take a deep breath and inhale; it doesn't have that musty male scent to it so I figure I'm safe to use it. I quickly rinse off and step out of the shower wrapping myself up in a fluffy white towel.

I riffle through my bag and pull out the new black silk and lace bra and panties that I bought today especially for tonight. They're hands down the sexiest piece of clothing I own. I figure boy shorts and a sports bra will kill the mood, so I slip the tiny scraps of fabric into place and then instantly feel self-conscious as I look at myself in the mirror. I could have sworn there was more to them when I'd tried them on in the store earlier.

I can feel my heart rate starting to pick up and my breathing becoming erratic as I pull my hair free and comb it through with my fingers. My hands are shaking and I clench and unclench my firsts a few times to try and relax.

Okay, this is only Ethan. I open the door and peek my head out.

The breath I was fighting to control a second ago is completely stolen as my eyes land on Ethan's back. He's standing at his dresser in nothing but a towel wrapped low around his waist. Beads of water are still glistening across his wide shoulders and taught muscular back. Suddenly my mouth feels extremely dry; maybe because it's hanging wide open while I'm standing in the doorway staring like a moron.

He reaches into one of the drawers and pulls out a pair of black boxers, and as he lets the towel fall I almost do, too. HOLY SHIT!

I gasp involuntarily and his head whips round, his eyes crashing into mine. His mouth quirks up on one side and he smirks before pulling his boxers on ridiculously slow. He knows he's putting on a show and I can't deny that I'm loving every moment of it. He lets the elastic at the top snap against the tight tanned skin leading down to his crazy hot V. I lean forward like a pervert, trying to get a closer look and the door swings open as I stumble through it. He laughs for a nanosecond before his eyes widen and his jaw goes slack. I stiffen and pull my arms across my chest and crotch trying to shield myself and turn around, expecting someone to be standing behind me, given the shocked look on Ethan's face.

I snap my head back to him in confusion; there's only us here, unless I'm missing something.

"Wow, Princess! You look…shit I don't even know a word that describes how perfect you look." I force my arms to drop. I want to keep them where they are and try cover myself but I know it doesn't exactly scream sexy and for once in my life I'd like to not act as awkward as I feel.

His gaze drops from my face to my chest and then begins a painfully slow descent down my body. The look on his face has me squeezing my legs together and goose bumps forming all over my skin. He slowly forces his eyes back up to mine and there's fire dancing in them. I don't know whether to be relieved that he seems to be enjoying the view or absolutely terrified of the look he's wearing.

He moves like a panther stalking its prey as he walks towards me and I take in each delicious dip of his abs as he draws closer.

"Be gentle with me." *Be gentle with me*—oh my god-—who would say that? Well, apparently me, I've just said that!

"I promise," he says in a low sexy voice that's now responsible for the fire burning in my panties.

He stops a few inches from my body; I can feel the heat of his skin radiating against mine and his breath rush-es across my face as he presses a kiss so light to my temple I barely feel it. Before I know what's happening he lifts me up, taking me by surprise, and my legs instantly wrap around his waist. I can feel his excitement underneath me and feel a sense of pride that I have this effect on him. I know that I'm not his first but I'm determined to be his last.

He walks us over to his bed and lays me down in the

center. I hold my breath in anticipation as he leans over me and claims my mouth, his tongue seeking permission against my lips to move with mine. He slides his hands into my hair and deepens the kiss. I have no control over the embarrassingly loud moan I let out and feel his smile against my lips.

His hands are everywhere all of a sudden and his kisses make their way from my lips, down my neck and across my chest, leaving a trail of fire in their wake. He pushes the lacy material from my breast and sucks my nipple into his mouth, flicking it with his tongue. I arch into him shamelessly as the sensation stirs the ache that's building in the pit of my stomach. I watch transfixed as he pulls his head back and makes a popping noise as the suction breaks. He leans over to show my other breast the same affection and my whole body tightens at the feel of it. My fingers push through his hair as I tug on it, writhing in pleasure under him. I watch him smile as he lifts and runs both of his hands across my chest and down over my stomach, making their way down to my panties. I lift my ass off the bed slightly and he grins as his fingers hook onto the sides and pull them down in one fluid movement.

"You're so perfect, Blair," he whispers just as his mouth collides with my core. I flinch at the contact and then abruptly grab hold of the sheets and will myself not to scream out at how good it feels. I throw my head back as his tongue tortures my clit in the most delicious way. I can feel my orgasm building as he kisses and licks, I can't concentrate on anything other than desperately trying to satisfy the need he's causing. He lifts his head and slides a finger inside of me before he goes back to circling my clit with his tongue, and that's all I need as my body tenses and then my orgasm hits with an overwhelming force. Wave after beautiful wave, making me feel like I'm about to explode into a thousand tiny pieces underneath him. He groans as my body tightens around him and it's the sexiest noise I've ever heard.

"Princess?" My eyes snap open and down to meet his, peeking up from between my legs. He stands and then leans across me and opens the drawer of his bedside table, retrieving a condom.

He straightens and smiles down at my boneless spent body. "We don't have to go any further than this, you know."

I lift myself up onto my elbows and lick my lips, I take in his flushed cheeks and messy dark hair, the intensity of his ice blue eyes as they focus on mine. My nerves seem to have disappeared and I know with absolute clarity that I want him. How can I not?

"I want to," I tell him, and it's the truth. I want him to make love to me more than I want my next breath.

He pushes the waistband of his boxers down and his erection springs free as he steps out of them. The image of his manhood has been ingrained in my mind since that day at the lake, but I can see that I definitely got the dimensions wrong. I thought he looked big at the lake, but standing here in front of me now with no cold-water taking effect, he's huge.

"I don't think you'll fit," I blurt out in a panic-stricken breath. "I thought you were smaller than that——it won't work."

The low rumble of laughter from his chest snaps me out of my meltdown and my eyes zero in on the condom he's rolling slowly down his shaft.

"It will," he replies and then winks, *freaking winks*, like this isn't a serious matter.

"Baby, you're not listening to me, it really won't."

He smirks and leans over placing a soft kiss onto my lips.

"Do you trust me Blair?"

"What?"

"Do you trust me?"

"Of course I trust you, it's ju—"

He places his finger over my lips to shush me.

"It will fit, I promise. It may hurt a little, but I'll be as gentle and slow as I can until you tell me otherwise. Okay?"

His hands press into the bed on either side of my face as he holds himself above me and I notice he's lost a little of the cockiness now. He's trembling and it suddenly dawns on me that he's nervous, too.

"I'm ready," I whisper, and he dips his head and kisses me. I move my lips against his and try to portray as much passion and desire as I can. I need this kiss to say the three little words that I know that I'm feeling, but haven't dared to voice. I. Love. You.

I feel him press lightly at my entrance and I panic. "Stop, wait…Just do it quickly, okay? I know it's gonna hurt, so just push in quick, like ripping off a band aid."

"Um…okay, are you sure, Princess?" he asks, looking unsure of himself.

"Yeah babe, jus—" I haven't even finished my sentence before he's thrust himself inside of me. "Holy shit! Ouch, ouch! Fuck, stop!" Pain is coursing through my vagina like nothing I've ever experienced before. "Shit, I didn't think it would sting. Is it supposed to sting?"

"I'm sorry, Princess, you told me to do it quick. Just try and relax, you'll adjust to my size in a second. I promise I won't move." He looks genuinely sorry and worried that he's hurting me and it makes me love him all the more. He's holding perfectly still and although it's hurting like hell, a noise escapes me that's half pained sob and half giggle. His eyes narrow and he pulls his head back ever so slightly.

"Are you okay?"

"I think so," I reply and then tilt my hips slightly. His eyes look like they're about to roll back into his head as a low growl escapes him.

"Fuck, Blair, when you do that it makes me really need to move." His voice sounds almost as pained as mine, only I can tell he's trying hard to use restraint.

I rock my hips forward a tiny bit and look into his eyes. "You can move slowly," I tell him as he dips his head and rests his forehead against mine.

Gradually my muscles seem to relax around him and the pain is replaced with a slow building pleasure as he slides gently in and out of me. Our bodies are slick with sweat as we glide against one another. I push my fingers into his back and moan his name as his pace begins to quicken.

"God yes, that feels so good baby," I exhale, reveling in the feeling. My groans seem to work Ethan into a passion educed frenzy, prompting his body to slam hungrily into mine. "Ethan, Harder!" I scream as he thrusts deeper and deeper inside of me and I can feel myself building again.

"Princess, I need you to come for me, you feel too good, I can't hold on." His voice almost sounds pained as he's pounding into me hard and fast. His fingers are tugging my hair as he thrusts deeper. I feel a red hot wave move across my body before I explode around him with an infinitely more intense sensation than I had when I came before. "Oh god, Ethan, I'm…I'm coming," I gasp as my orgasm sends lights shooting behind my eyes as my body tingles and clamps down around him.

"Fuck, Blair," he growls as he finds his own release, and him throbbing inside of me sends a new wave of aftershocks through me, making me tighten around him again and again. It's pure ecstasy; every nerve in my body is alive as heat crashes over me.

Ethan's body relaxes and drapes over mine, our breathing slowing from the erratic panting of just moments ago. I'm limp and exhausted in the very best way. I want to stay like this forever.

"Blair?" he whispers so softly as he pulls out of me and I barely register the sound.

"Yeah?" I breathe out. My eyes are heavy with contentment and I can't remember a time I ever felt this sated.

"Can I keep you?"

I smile as I let out a long exhale. "Only forever."

"Promise?"

"Cross my heart," I tell him as my eyelids drop and I let sleep claim me.

Chapter 28

Ethan

I WALK BACK from the bathroom and Blair's asleep. I stand over the bed and stare at her in awe. She's laid on her stomach and her messy sex hair is fanned out over my pillows. It's the hottest sight I've ever seen, she's breathtaking. The sheets are tangled up around her and only covering one half of her body, a perfectly toned leg leading up to one perfectly curved ass cheek is on display and the sight has me ready for round two.

I climb into the bed beside her and pull her naked body flush with mine so I'm spooning her. Her soft ass wriggles back against my dick as I envelope my body around hers, my arms encasing her and cupping her breasts. I push my face through her hair and rest my chin on her shoulder. I couldn't be any closer to her and yet I still don't feel close enough. I squeeze her ever so slightly and she wriggles her body back again.

"Mmm, you feel too good to be true," she says, her

voice thick with sleep.

I smile into her neck as her words wash over me; I've never felt as relaxed as I do right now. Things make more sense when she's with me. My life feels easier, my worries seem less of a burden and I want so badly to tell her that I love her. I need to stop myself from speaking the words right now. I don't want her to think I'm saying it because we've just had sex, and it's the thing to do. When I tell her, I need her to be completely sure that I'm saying it because there's never been anything truer.

I can't picture a future without her in it now. I've had a taste of what my life could be like, what my life should be like and I can't ignore it. I can't go back to the numbness. She's under my skin; her essence is running through my veins and taking a hold of my heart. She owns me in every way a person can be owned and when I finally tell her those three little words, I need her to understand the place where they're coming from. Maybe if I hadn't experienced so many dark moments with my father, I would have never noticed Blair shining. But looking down at this beautiful girl asleep beside me now, I know I wouldn't change a single thing about my past, because it brought me my future.

elle

"Ethan?" I'm jolted awake as Blair pushes against my arm still trapping her body against mine.

"Mm."

She pushes again, harder to garner more of a response, but I don't want to move, she feels too good pressed against me.

"Ethan, we need to get up. We fell asleep and didn't set an alarm. What time is it?"

I groan and stretch my arms over my head and then reach behind me, feeling around on my nightstand for my phone. I press the button and the home screen lights up letting me know it's only 5:15am.

"Ugh, it's still early, Princess," I say, waving my phone in front of her so she can see.

She twists her body around so she's facing me. "Sorry baby, I woke up and panicked that we'd slept too long."

"What does it matter?" I ask pulling her close so her body is flush with mine. My morning wood is pressed against her warm stomach. Her eyes widen a little before they burn bright with desire and my body instantly awakens.

"How are you feeling downstairs?"

A blush spreads like wildfire over her cheeks and down her neck as she rubs her legs together a little.

"I think I'm good, a little sore. I kind of feel like I've just done a really long bike ride," she says with a coy grin. "Sort of like you're still in me, maybe."

It shouldn't please me that I've left her feeling that way, but the asshole inside of me doe's a little fist pump.

"You think you could handle doing it again?" I ask against her lips as I part them and push my tongue inside her mouth. She kisses back for a second before her eyes widen and she jumps back like I've just thrown ice over her.

"I need to go brush my teeth." Her eyes are wide and she clamps her hand across her mouth.

I can't suppress the chuckle that bubbles from my chest as I pull her face back to mine.

"I don't care," I tell her between little kisses.

I feel her shoulders relax as she lets me kiss her how I want to. I take the little mewing sounds coming from her as a green light.

I fumble in the bedside cabinet grabbing a handful of condoms without breaking our kiss, and drop them onto the bed next to us.

"You're confident," she splutters out, and I laugh with her.

"Not confident, more like hopeful, really, really hope-ful." I tear open one of the little packages and go to put it on.

"Can I do that?"

Fuck yeah, she can! I feel myself harden even more as she's looking up at me through her lashes, biting that sweet plump bottom lip of hers.

I pass her the condom and she takes it with a flirta-tious little smirk and begins rolling it down over me. Her small hands curl around the base of me as she draws me closer to her and the sight makes me groan.

"Will it hurt as much as last time?" she asks and I still myself at her entrance. Truth is I'm not sure; I've popped a few girls' cherries but never stuck around afterwards. It's always been a case of fucking them and leaving before the condom hits the bottom of the trashcan.

"I don't think so, I'll take it nice and slow this time," I tell her as I push inside of her as slowly as I can bear. She's so tight I could blow before I'm even all the way in.

She lets out a gasp but then her body starts to relax around me and I push a little further.

"Does that feel okay?" I'm suddenly worried that I'm hurting her again; her satisfied smile eases my conscious.

"It feels a whole lot better than okay, Ethan," she tells me as her fingernails bite into my ass. "Let's just stay here and do this forever."

I rock into her, finally pushing all the way in and I can't think of anything else I'd rather do forever than this.

"Deal," I tell her as I find a steady rhythm and spend the next hour making slow sweet love to my girl.

Chapter 29

Blair

"DOES THIS SAY 'cute and fun', or 'trying too hard'?" Brie asks as she holds a skirt to herself in the mirror of the store we've been in for the last forty minutes.

"Trying too hard!" Casey and I say at the same time. I'm pretty sure I have panties that cover more than the skirt she's holding up.

"Really? Huh, I think it's cute," she says, swaying it from side to side.

"Brie! We have been in here foreverrrr. Can we go already?" I'm tired and weighed down with a million and one bags. I usually shop on my own, hit a couple of stores and bam, I'm done. Shopping with Brie and Casey is a whole different ball game. I didn't realize that there were actually this many stores in the mall, and I think we've been in some twice. If shopping were an Olympic sport, these girls would be in the running for gold.

I'm like a fish out of water when I shop. I smile as I

remember one of the last times Em and I went to the mall together.

Em was in a changing room trying on jeans and called me to come in and give her my opinion. I pulled the curtain back and Emily was standing with a scowl on her face.

"This is ridiculous, the steroids have made me lose so much weight, I have the body of a twelve-year-old boy! Seriously, look at this," she motioned to her ass where the jeans were completely baggy and hanging funny. "I should just buy a pair of Calvin's and walk around with my ass hanging out like a skater boy."

I suppressed a laugh and scrunched my nose. "Yep, those are definitely not the right cut for you anymore. Shame though, they're cute."

"You should take them and try them on, they'd look good on you," she said, slipping the jeans down her legs and shoving them into my arms.

"Sure you don't mind?"

"Why would I mind?"

"Just you really liked them, is all." I looked at her for confirmation and she just shook her head.

"You're strange sometimes; of course I don't mind."

"Okay, then."

I unbuckled my belt and wiggled out of my shorts before shaking out the jeans in front of me. I pulled the jeans up my calves and over my knees. The denim didn't have much give and I did a little jump and held onto the belt loops as I tried to hoist them up. It wasn't happening, though, and the jump set me off balance. I fell slightly into the side of the cubicle and then everything seemed to happen in slow motion. The rail holding the curtain slipped from its mount and came crashing down, while at the same time one side of the cubicle collapsed and crashed into the next. We both watched in horror at the domino effect, one by one the five cubicles in the women's changing room came crashing down around us. It sounded like a bomb being detonated. Em took one look at my panic-stricken face and burst out laughing.

The sales assistants came running through to see what had happened, men and women both. They came to an abrupt stop and surveyed the sight that greeted them. Em was sitting amongst the curtains on the store floor in fits of laughter, tears streaming down her pretty face as I was standing frozen in the middle of the room, clutching a pair of jeans that I couldn't pull past my thighs. To make matters worse, I was wearing a bright blue thong that had the word ANGRY above a picture of a cartoon beaver. I glanced behind me and realized that every mirror in the dressing room was doing a pretty stellar job of reflecting my thong-clad ass.

I smile about it now, but at the time it was the most horrifically awkward shopping trip I'd ever been on. There really is no wonder why I don't like shopping.

"Jeez, Blair, are you sure you're a girl? You complain more than my brother does when Lauren drags him shopping," Brie says with her hand on her hip, pouting.

"Sorry, I'm just tired," I tell them, and right on cue I let out a huge yawn.

"Someone keep you up all night?" Casey wiggles her eyebrows at me and I feel the embarrassment wash straight over my face, heating my cheeks.

"Holy shit, you're blushing, did you and Ethan bump uglies?" Brie laughs, hanging the skirt she's holding on the nearest rack and marching over to me.

I groan in anticipation of the twenty questions she's sure to throw at me.

"You did, didn't you? Ha-ha! I knew it! Didn't I say that they'd end up having sex last night, Case?" She nods at Casey in encouragement and continues. "So come on, dish it, was it good? Is he big? Did he get you off? I wanna know everything."

I look around the store, mortified at how loud she just asked that, and then whisper-shout at her, "I'm not telling you that, especially not in here!" I motion with my hand wildly around us at the store full of people.

"Chill, nobody knows you, they won't care," Casey drops in and both girls nod their heads at me, eager for my admissions.

"Not. A. Chance!"

"Fine!" Brie says with a pout. "Let's go grab a coffee and you can tells us then."

I shake my head at her, but still follow them out of the store and down the escalators to the coffee shop on the first floor.

ele

We settle into the plush warm brown leather sofas with mochas in hand and then I wait for the onslaught to begin. An awkward silence settles among us as they sit facing me, eyes wide and waiting to be regaled with the events of my night with Ethan.

"You're kind of freaking me out guys," I admit and Brie lets out an exasperated sigh.

"Fine, we'll do this the hard way." My gaze narrows as I look at her in confusion. She takes a sip of her drink and places it on the table in front of us.

"Okay, so you slept with Ethan last night, correct?"

There's no way they would believe me if I denied it, so I go with the truth.

"Yes."

"And?"

"And what?"

"Oh, for fuck's sake, you're killing me here! And how was it?" she asks, looking at me like I'm a moron.

I smile at the memory of last night and this morning. "Pretty amazing, actually."

Brie finally smiles, satisfied with my answer as Casey interjects. "I hate you a little right now. I bet he was huge, too, wasn't he? Please tell me no! A boy that good looking, popular and in a freaking band can't be blessed with being hung like a stallion too, surely?"

Brie and I fall back into the sofa laughing as Casey shakes her head in disappointment.

"He is, isn't he? Damn, he doesn't happen to have some long lost brother out there, does he?"

"DIBS IF HE HAS!" Brie practically screams, and the older couple sitting at the table across from us shoots death glares as they're wiping up the coffee they'd spilled at Brie's outburst.

"Okay, so I'm not giving you the sordid details. Sorry, but it's not happening. All you're getting is that it happened and it was amazing. That's it, end of discussion."

"You suck," Brie says with a huge grin, and then, just like that, the conversation switches to the purchases we've just made, and what shirt to wear with which pair of pants. I relax into the sofa with my mocha and fight the urge to go to sleep.

ele

"Blair, is that you?" my mom calls as I struggle to get through the front door with all my shopping bags. I'd rather risk my wrists breaking than have to make two trips.

"Yeah, it's me." I burst through the door into the family room and drop myself onto the sofa dramatically, letting the bags fall at my feet.

"Hard day's shopping?" she says with a surprised look.

"I'm never going to the mall with Brie and Casey again; it was like some mad endurance challenge or something!"

Mom laughs and shakes her head. "Ah you just take after your father, if I was in a store longer than five minutes he'd complain."

"Yeah, well Dad was a smart man."

She smiles warmly at the memory. "So, I'm guessing you were buying stuff for your trip with Ethan. I don't see any Agent Provocateur bags; I guess I can sleep easy tonight."

It's one of those moments when you really don't know how to act: do I laugh and joke with her that it's hidden in another bag, or do I panic and bail? I'm thinking the latter when she laughs at me.

"Relax, Blair, I was joking. How was the party?"

This is where I need to decide whether or not to confide in her that I lost my virginity. When I was younger, Mom and I were really close, much more so than we are now. When I hit fourteen and got my period, my hormones were all over the place and the doctors suggested I start on birth control to regulate it. Mom decided to my complete and utter embarrassment that she should give me the sex talk. We made a pact that when I did lose my virginity, (and if it was before I was legal she'd kill me!) I would tell her. I always thought that I probably wouldn't, but agreed to it anyway. Now that the moments arrived, I feel a strange urge to keep my promise.

I take a deep breath and look her in the eyes. She smiles softly at me; it's a knowing smile, one that tells me she knows what I'm about to say.

"Ethan and I slept together." I blurt the words out as if they're burning my throat.

"Thank you for telling me that, sweetheart." I can't tell if the emotion I'm seeing is sadness that I've had sex, or admiration that I actually kept my promise and told her.

She crosses the room and takes a seat next to me, pulling me in for a hug and she grips me so tightly it feels like she's worried I might disappear. She sniffs and I realize that she's crying. My stomach bottoms out and I pull back and look at her.

"I'm sorry if I've disappointed you bu—" she cuts me off shaking her head.

"Blair, you haven't disappointed me at all. I'm crying because I'm a silly emotional old woman who just realized her baby's not a baby anymore, no matter how much I wish she was." Her breathing stutters and she wipes at the corner of her eyes. "You did use protection, right?"

"Yes, we used protection, Mom."

"Good girl, I hope he realizes the gift you've given him. I'll put a hit out on him if he breaks your heart."

I laugh and she pulls me back against her and cuddles me once more. It's my turn to start crying now and she smiles at me. "Look at the two of us. We must look crazy."

"Who cares," I say. "I love you."

"Aw, sweetheart, I love you too—so, so much." She pats my back and then stands.

"Come on then, let me help you take these bags to your room."

I sigh as I realize that for all her faults, and all of mine, for that matter, I'm pretty blessed to have this woman as my mom.

ele

Mom left me to put away the clothes I was railroaded into buying with Casey and Brie. I'm now sitting at my desk staring down at Emily's list. I'm poised with pen in hand, ready to cross off #10. Lose my V card (Ideally Ethan Jamison!) The irony that he is actually my boyfriend is not lost on me.

I put a strike through it and then sit and stare for seconds, minutes—hours, maybe, who knows? It doesn't look right. It doesn't feel right. I shouldn't be crossing off sleeping with my own boyfriend. It's far too personal, too intimate. The only list Ethan belongs on is my own. I fold it up and place it back in its spot, making a mental note that once The Grand Canyon and Vegas are crossed off, the list is done. I refuse to cross off anything else having to do with Ethan.

I look at the picture of Em and me that's sitting in a frame on my desk. I pick it up and touch the image. "Sorry Em," I whisper into the empty room. "You're going to have to haunt my ass, I can't cross off Ethan on your list, but I'll cross everything else for you. Please don't be mad. I miss you." I replace the picture and lie across my bed. The last twenty-four hours have been intense and I feel completely drained, physically and mentally. I smile to myself thinking I wouldn't change it. Not one single thing.

Ethan

I'M RUNNING LATE to collect Blair, a group of us are meeting at the movie theatre and I told her I'd be there to pick her up five minutes ago. I shrug into my jacket and grab my keys from the counter.

"I'm going out, Mom, I have a key if you wanna lock up!" I shout as I'm almost out the door. I hear her shouting for me to wait and then she rushes to the hall flustered as I look down at my phone to check the time again.

"I'm late, Mom, what is it?"

An expression passes over her face that I can't read. "Ethan, I really need to talk to you." Her voice shakes as she says it.

"Can we talk after—"

"No, this can't wait, I've been putting it off long enough and I want to speak with you before your father gets home." She turns and walks back into the kitchen and I follow. Whatever it is that she wants to tell me can't be

203

good; she looks as though she wants to throw up and my mind suddenly starts racing with all the terrible things she could potentially be about to tell me.

She sits at the table and I take the seat opposite, the air around us thickening with tension with every passing second. I have a really bad feeling about this; I almost don't want to ask but I do anyway.

"So, what is it you need to talk to me about?"

She places her clasped hands out in front of her on the table and I notice they're trembling. Shit.

"Honey...I need you to just remember that what I'm about to tell you, I did for your own good. At least that's what I thought I was doing." She pinches the bridge of her nose between her thumb and forefinger. I'm officially now freaking the fuck out. I'm waiting for her to tell me she's dying or something.

Her eyes glaze over with unshed tears and I'm holding my breath waiting for the news.

"Fuck, Mom, what is it? You're scaring me now!"

She takes a breath and regains her composure; sitting straight in her chair and looking me square in the eyes.

"Ethan honey, I'm not your mother."

I don't know if I've heard her wrong or if she's muddled her words but they make no fucking sense. She can see my obvious confusion and takes it as her cue to clarify.

"I met your father when you were seven months old, your Mom—his fiancé at the time—died of a brain hemorrhage when she was in labor with you."

I'm still holding my breath and my lungs start to burn, the sensation reminds me to breathe. My head's swimming with the revelation and I feel dizzy and disorientated.

I stand and move away from the table to try and regain my equilibrium; the sudden movement makes my
head feel worse. My step falters and I rest myself against
the island and try to take a few deep breaths. Mom, or at
least the woman I've been calling Mom my whole fucking
existence, swiftly jumps up and reaches out to steady me.

"Don't!" I bite out and sit back down at the table. I
don't want her to touch me, her feeble attempt at comfort.
I just want the truth.

"This is bullshit! Why are you telling me this now?"

"Ethan, I've loved you from the very first second I set
my eyes on you. I started dating your father while he was
struggling to look after you by himself with no help. He
was a mess. He'd just lost the woman he was going to
marry and gained a baby he knew absolutely nothing about
how to handle. We were married just before your first
birthday and my parents said I was mad. They didn't ap-
prove of our relationship. My mother told me he was only
marrying me to offload you, and well, that was that. They
made it perfectly clear that they didn't want anything to do
with my new family or me so I broke all contact with
them. I married your dad and started raising you as my
own." Her tears are running silently down her face as she's
confessing that my life to date has been nothing but one
huge lie.

"He wasn't always so angry and bitter, you know.
There was a time when we were all happy, for a short
while at least."

"Really? Because I sure as hell don't remember it!" I
snap at her and my words make her flinch and recoil back
in her seat.

"You started getting older and your dad started growing more and more distant. He told me that you reminded him of Samantha, your mom. Your looks, your mannerisms, they all started to grate on him. He became more and more angry as time went on. He was always so busy with work and stressed constantly. I told him I was leaving him the first time he ever hit you. You were about seven years old. You'd been playing in the garden and came in dirty and ran mud through the house with your soccer boots on. It was like a switch flipped in his head; he hit you so hard I was sure he'd broken your arm. That night, I packed up a bag for us and was fastening you into the car when he came home early. He dragged me into the house and beat the living crap out of me for trying to steal you. Told me that if I ever tried to leave with you again, he would kill me. You have to believe me, Ethan, I didn't doubt him for a second. I've wanted to leave him every single day from then on. The only reason I'm here now is you. I couldn't leave you by yourself with him. Even if I had managed to get us away, legally you're his and not mine."

My eyes are blurry from my own tears that I'm trying my damnedest to hold on to. I don't know how to respond to what she's telling me. I'm beyond pissed that she's kept this from me for eighteen years, but a part of me feels sorry for her too. I'm all fucked up and confused and I wish like hell Blair was here with me now. She'd know what to say to help me process this; she always makes me feel better.

"You just let him beat me, though. You stayed, but what for? You never helped me."

The sob that she lets out cuts straight through me. It's the sound of complete devastation and a lifetime of regret.

She's fighting hard to steady her breathing so she can speak but I've heard enough, I don't want to know anymore. I want to shut down my mind, hit a pause button and just take a second to gather my racing thoughts.

"Ethan, I wish every day that I'd told someone, gotten help. But who would have helped me? He's a policeman, for god's sake; he's connected. He could and would have covered up whatever allegations I made. Where would that have left us, then? He sure as hell wouldn't let me take you away. At least by being here with you, in my mind I was protecting you."

"So why the sudden urge to tell me all this, huh? If you're so scared of him and what he'll do, why are you telling me this now?" I'm tense as hell as I wait for her to reply.

"I'm telling you now because you're eighteen. I've wanted to tell you every day since your birthday and I've never had the chance, found the right moment, or had the courage, I guess. You're a legal adult now; he has no real bearing over you. When you start college I'm leaving him. With you gone there's nothing left for me here but a terrible marriage to a monstrous man. I needed you to know the real reasons why I'm leaving, so you don't think that I've just abandoned you."

My voice finally cracks and the tears win out, they race down my face and the more I try to wipe at them, the more they seem to fall.

My phone starts to ring in my back pocket; it's more than likely Blair wanting to know what's taking me so long. I can't answer in the state I'm in— I don't want to scare her. I let it go to voice mail and Mom walks around the table and places her arms around me. I throw my arms around her tightly and cry into her shoulder, like a five-year-old that's scraped his knee and needs his mom. I can't remember the last time that I ever held her like this.

She's rubbing circles on my back and making a shushing noise into my shoulder.

"You'll never know how sorry I am that I've let you live this life, Ethan. I've let you down in every way a person can and I hate myself for it."

The whole twisted fucked-up situation feels like a weight that I can't hold onto, it's dragging me down like quicksand and I'm sinking so fast it's beginning to suffocate me. I need some fresh air; I need to get out of this house. I need Blair.

"I have to go, I can't be here. I need to leave." I'm in a panic and Mom's eyes widen as she moves back from me.

"I know this is a lot to take in, honey, but your father will be home tonight. We need to make out that everything is normal. It's only a couple of weeks until graduation, then you'll be at college before you know it."

"Are you fucking kidding me right now?" I stand, the anxiety and suffocating now morphing instantly into pure rage. "You seriously expected to tell me this and then have me act like everything is normal?"

"Ethan calm down please hon—"

I cut her off shouting before she can finish.

"Jesus Christ, Mom, have you heard yourself? Calm down? How can you be seriously saying this to me!"

She straightens and regains her self-control.

"Ethan, listen to me. You need to act normal for your own good. I need you to keep your cool and everything

208

can go ahead like I've planned it."

"What do mean 'like you've planned it', planned what?" I ask incredulously.

She takes a deep breath and carries on. "Once your scholarship's confirmed and I know the balance of your tuition, I can use the money in our savings account to pay the whole thing off. There should be a little left over to get you by, but it would probably be wise for you to get a part-time job to subsidize it. As soon as the money clears you'll be fine. You won't need your father or me for anything. We can both break free of him."

I stop pacing and stare at her blankly. She actually thinks this is going to work; I can see it on her face.

"If he finds out about this, Ethan, I don't know what he'll do but it will be bad, I can promise you that."

I shake my head. I'm done. I need to leave now; it's all just too much to take in.

"I'm going to Blair's...I can't handle this," I tell her, ignoring her pleas as I pass her and walk straight out to my car without looking back.

My life is one giant clusterfuck. I need to go and see the only thing that I've ever managed to get right. I turn the key in the ignition and pull out of my drive. I need to go find Blair.

Chapter 31

Blair

"HI IT'S ETHAN, you know what to do...Beep" I end the
call again. I've already left a voice message and sent two
texts. At this point I feel like I'm bordering on stalker sta-
tus, but it's not like him to make plans and then just bail
without word. He knows how much I hate that. I decide
that I should just call Casey and catch a ride with her to the
movie theater; Ethan can meet me there if he ever decides
to get back to me. I call Casey and ten minutes later we're
en route.

"So what, he just didn't show up?" she asks as we
turn off my street.

"Yeah, he's not answering his calls or my texts, either. Hopefully he'll call me back soon."

"I'm sure he will," she says, but I have a sinking feeling in the pit of my stomach.

What if something's happened with his dad? I should
have just driven over to his house; instead, I've stranded

myself without a car by riding with Casey. The more I think about it the more panicked and convinced I am that I'm correct. God, I hope I'm not.

We make idle small talk until we reach the movie theater. I'm anxious and I think she can tell. We stand in line to buy our tickets as the others spot us and make their way over. My eyes do a quick scan of the group but I can't see Ethan with them.

I sigh audibly as Jackson reaches my side.

"Gee thanks, nice to see you too." He sounds offended but when I look up, his lips are quirked up at the corners and I realize he's just teasing.

"Sorry Jackson, you know I'm always happy to see you. Hey, has Ethan been in touch with you? He was supposed to be picking me up but he never showed. I had to catch a ride with Casey." I motion over to where Casey and Brie are standing, studying the different ice creams at the B&J counter.

"Nah, sorry, I ain't spoken to him today."

"Okay, never mind." I attempt to smile but it's forced as we head to our screen.

The opening credits have just started when I feel my cell vibrating in my purse. I pull it out to see it's Ethan calling and I don't think twice as I press accept and say hello. The whole theater throws glares at me and some guy shouts out that cell phones aren't allowed to be on in here. I resist the urge to flip him off as I whisper into the receiver for Ethan to hold on.

I make my way down the row of chairs, all of the annoyed moviegoers looking like they want to kill me for making them move so that I can squeeze my way out. I'm almost at the end when I kick a guy's drink over.

"Shoot! I'm so sorry," I say to him and we both bend at the same time to pick up the cup. We smack heads so hard that I'm pretty sure I really do see stars. We both bring our hands up to our heads and I knock his popcorn from his other hand.

"Jesus, you should come with a health warning!" he snaps, and my cheeks start burning. I can hear Ethan shouting down my cell, asking what's going on and am I alright.

I apologize to the guy and offer to pay for his food and drink but he just shakes his head and shoos me away. I step out into the aisle and make my way to the exit so I can finally take Ethan's call.

"Okay, sorry about that baby. Where are you? The movie's already started, what happened?"

"Sorry Princess, something came up. I'm outside the movie theater now; do you think you could come out?" His voice sounds scratchy and fear courses through my veins. My mind instantly goes to what his dad may have done to him. My stomach knots at the thought and I have to work at keeping my voice steady.

"I'll be right out; I just need to go grab my things and let the others know I'm leaving. Ethan…are you hurt?" I need to prepare my mind in case I get outside and he looks a mess. My poker face sucks.

"Not the way you're thinking." *Not the way I'm thinking*, what the hell does that mean?

"Okay, I'll be right out." I disconnect the call and rush back to collect my belongings.

ele

I step outside the theater and notice Ethan's car idling at the curb. I pull my jacket tightly around me like a shield against what I might be about to see. I'm not normally so pessimistic in my thoughts; I like to think I'm a glass half-full kind of person, but when it comes to Ethan's home life, I can't help but assume the worst. I pull the car door open and slip inside, angling my body towards his. I scan him instantly looking for any signs that he's been hurt but I can't see any.

"Hey beautiful, you're a sight for sore eyes," he tells me as he leans in and kisses me softly on the lips. He holds us pressed together for a few beats before he pulls back, cupping my face with his hands. His mood is definitely off but I can't pinpoint how.

"Baby, are you okay?"

He sighs and looks at me, his normally clear blue eyes look cloudy and are rimmed red. I realize he's been crying and it makes my heart sink as I'm waiting for him to answer me.

"I am now," he whispers and then moves back and replaces his seat belt. "Buckle up, Princess, we'll go somewhere to talk."

"Okay," I smile at him and try to portray a confidence that I am just not feeling.

ele

We drive in silence to the beach. We park and he

leads me by the hand down to the warm soft sand. It's almost silent except for the noise of waves crashing against the shore as we sit facing out to the ocean. I stay quiet, allowing him the time to work out what it is that he wants to say to me.

"So today my mom told me that she's not actually my mom."

I'm drawing patterns in the sand with my fingers and I still at his words.

"Apparently my real mom died when she was having me."

I'm completely taken aback, stunned, mute. Hell, if we weren't already both sitting down I think I would have just fallen over with the force of that omission. How could they not have told him before now?

I throw my arms around him and pull him to me as tightly as I can. It's not a selfless act. It provides just as much a comfort for me as I hope it does for him.

"Shit, Ethan I don't know what to say."

"That's not even the best part." He lets out a humorless laugh. "Mom seems to think that me reminding Dad of my birth mom is the reason he is the way he is."

"Wait, what? She said that?" I don't know if I'm reading it wrong but it sounds like he just told me that his dad beats him for just existing as himself. He can't control being like someone he's never met. How on earth can he be punished for something so out of his control? I have a fiercely strong dislike of Ethan's dad at the best of times, but hearing this, I know without a doubt in my mind that it's no longer a dislike; it's pure hate.

"You do know that it's not your fault, baby. You've done nothing to deserve the way he treats you."

He smiles a sad smile and kisses my temple. I know that he doesn't believe me and that's the problem. He's spent so long being told he's a worthless disappointment, I'm not sure how to make him see the truth——that by just being here with me now makes him stronger than he'll ever know. He had the guts to tell me about his past. He hasn't just given up or run away or let his dad take away his plans for college and his life.

We sit for a long time, staring out at the ocean as he replays what happened today, reminiscing about things that have happened in the past that he's now seeing in a new light.

"I think I understand your mom a little better now," I say softly as I'm letting the sand that's now starting to turn cold with the setting sun, slips through my fingertips.

He's sitting forward with his elbows rested on his drawn-up knees, his head hung low studying the sand beneath him. He twists his head to look at me, confusion clear in his expression. "How do you mean?"

I draw my knees up and hug them to my chest as I rest my tilted head on them.

"When you first told me what was going on with your dad, I couldn't understand how your mom could let it happen. I can't imagine how a mother could ever stand back and let her child, someone she should love above every other living thing on this earth, be hurt like that. It made no sense to me. If I'm honest it's probably why I try to avoid her. Every time I see her I want to shake her and ask her why."

His eyes widen at my words and I blink away the tears I didn't realize had started pooling in my eyes.

"I understand her a little more now, knowing that she couldn't take you and get away from him. I still wish she had been stronger and had tried harder, but I get it." I feel a blanket of shame settle over me as I look into his beautiful blue eyes. "I'm just as guilty as her," I tell him as a sob escapes. His head snaps up, an emotion I can't read plays in his eyes as he waits for me to continue. "I know what's been going on and I've told no one. What kind of person does that make me, Ethan?"

"No, Blair, don't go there, Princess. I'm the asshole here for putting this shit on you and then making you hold onto it. My dad's right, I am a selfish little prick. I told you not to tell anyone, I made you promise. God, baby, if I'd known how much I was hurting you doing that…" He trails off, shaking his head. I watch his hands clench as he pounds his fist into the sand next to him, cussing before finally looking back to me.

"I'm sorry I've put this on you, you don't deserve this." He squeezes his eyes shut as a tear escapes and it all but breaks my already heavy heart.

The sight tips me over the edge and I cry, not just a few silent tears, but a real honest-to-god uncontrollable outburst. The look on his face makes me cry harder. He's apologizing to me and it's so fucked up. I'm the one who should be asking for his forgiveness. I've failed him.

He straightens his legs and pulls me into his lap. I cling onto his neck and cry into his shirt as he gently rocks us back and forth.

"It's me who should apologize, Ethan," I tell him when my breathing has calmed. "You have nothing to be sorry about, you've been dealt a completely horrendous hand in life. The people that should protect you haven't and you need to believe me when I tell you that it's not your fault. You can't think like that. Please trust what I'm telling you."

He squeezes me slightly burying his face in my hair. He kisses my head and then moves to place a kiss against my ear and then my jaw, making his way around to my lips. I can taste the saltiness of our tears and he cups my face and lets his lips fall from mine. Our foreheads are pressed together and I'm dizzy with the sensation of his kiss mingled with the emotional intensity of the moment.

"I love you," he breathes out so low that I can't be sure that I didn't just imagine it.

I pull my head back to look at him and before I can breathe a single word his lips are on mine again, moving so slow and tenderly that I know I heard him. I can feel the love that he's pouring into this kiss and I let it wash over me. My body melts against his as he drops his hands to my waist. He pulls me closer and then snakes them up and down my back. I'm not sure if we spend minutes or even hours like that, but when we pull away I'm breathless. I open my mouth to tell him that I feel the same but he speaks before I have a chance.

"I think I knew the moment I first noticed you sitting in the library waiting on me. You're like this amazingly beautifully blinding light that has drawn me out of my own darkness. I was living in a constant state of numbness and I thought it was fine to go on like that. I didn't realize it was possible for another person to make me feel the way that you do. You changed that for me. I love you so damn much."

I smile as he lifts me from his lap and then places me

in front of him and brushes the sand from my legs. I desperately want to tell him that I love him, too, but the words don't seem enough after his declaration. I need him to know that I'm not just saying it in response to him saying it first.

"Come on, Princess, it's getting cold, let's get back to the car." He takes my hand as we walk across the beach in silence. My mind is desperately trying to formulate the words to let him know, to show him that my feelings run so much deeper than what those three little words can describe. I need to make him feel the way he's just made me feel, and 'I love you' just doesn't seem adequate anymore.

Chapter 32

Ethan

I PULL UP to the curb and turn off the ignition. The drive back to Blair's has been mostly silent and subdued, the gravity of the day's events looming over us like a thick heavy black rain cloud.

"You can stay here tonight. I'm sure I can talk my mom into it, although it will mean you sleeping in the guest room?" she says, looking pensive.

I want to tell her yes, that I want nothing more than to stay here with her and not return to the messed up situation I walked away from a few hours ago. I know I can't, though. It would cause too many questions that I don't have answers for yet. As much as I hate the idea, I need to go home. I'll keep up the pretense that everything is normal until I can process this thing properly.

"I can't, Princess, I need to get back. Keep to the usual routine of what my dad expects." I can see the concern cross her face before she has time to mask it.

"I'll be fine, promise," I tell her with an air of confidence that doesn't match how I'm feeling right now. I can't bear the thought of her worrying herself over me. I want to be the person who makes her feel safe, makes her feel happy, makes her feel loved. Not the asshole that dumps all his baggage on her and brings her down. The more I'm with her, the more I'm becoming that person and I need to change that. She deserves someone better than me and if I weren't such a selfish prick, I'd let her go and find it. I am a selfish prick though, so I don't. I need her too much.

"Will you call me before you go to sleep tonight?"

"Sure I will…now, get going, it's getting late." I smile as I lean across to push her door open.

"You trying to get rid of me?"

"Yes!" I deadpan. "I'm late for another date."

She nips my side, making me jump.

"That's not funny." I'm sure she's trying to do her best pissed-off glare but she's ruining the effect with the slight grin tugging at her lips.

"It's not funny, you're right. She'll freak if I don't show." This time she nips me really fucking hard. "Argh, shit! Quit it, I'm sorry!" I'm wincing like a little bitch as she twists my nipple so hard it feels like it's coming off. She narrows her eyes this time and pushes her face right up to mine, so close that her breath fans across me when she speaks, her fingers still holding my contorted skin in her vice-like grip.

"Unless you're not particularly fond of this nipple, you'll take that back!"

"Fuck, Princess, I take it back, I take it back, just let go." She releases her fingers and my hand shoots instantly up to my chest, rubbing the affected area. "Christ, that stings."

She sits back into her seat with a self-satisfied smirk. "That'll teach you to tease me."

No shit it'll teach me, I think to myself. "You're mean but you're hot, so I'll let that slide." I place a chaste kiss on her lips, careful to keep my arm across my chest protecting my goods.

"Night, Blair, I love you." The words float from my lips like it's the most natural thing on earth to say to her. It feels right. Instead of the sudden sensation of fear and anxiety I thought might have happened, I feel comforted that she knows that I love her.

"Night baby." She doesn't say it back, and although I don't expect her to, or even want her to say it until she means it, it kind of stings.

ele

I've kept up with Mom's fake little happy family show she's been playing for my dad for the last few weeks. Blair and I are setting off for our trip in little over an hour, graduation is next week and then the end is in sight. Blair asks daily how everything is. My response is always the same: everything is going well; he doesn't suspect that anything is going on. This seems to calm her, satisfy the nervousness. It's not the truth, though, at least not the whole truth.

He doesn't know that Mom's confessed to me, but everything is far from fine. He's facing forced retirement at work and I'm his number one outlet for his frustrations.

I won't tell Blair that. The look on her face when she was crying at the beach will be forever etched in my mind. I refuse to ever make her look or feel that way again. If it means taking a few beatings and sucking it up, not telling anyone, then bring it on. I've done it for most my life. I'm good at it.

My car's packed up and ready to leave, I've more or less emptied the contents of the fridge into a cooler on my back seat, downloaded a ton of new songs for the drive and I'm good to go. My cell beeps and I read the message from Blair.

From: Princess
I've been packed for the last three hours!!!
Any chance you're about ready to go now?
I'm excited x

I smile to myself; I love that she's this eager to spend time with me. I reply telling her I'm on my way and leave a note for my mom on the refrigerator with the campsite address. I've had too many run-ins with my dad and know better than to leave and not let them know where I am or when I'll be back. The thought of being free of this house and all the bullshit that goes with it is a heady sensation. I jump in my car and feel the best that I have in a really long time, a full weekend alone with Blair is all I've thought about, it's what has gotten me thorough these last few weeks. My girl is like magic.

It takes all my effort not to laugh as Blair's mom gives us the 'safe sex' talk. Not because I think it's funny, but because it's so fucking awkward and apparently my brain's default setting in uncomfortable situations is to laugh. I'm studying the floor like it's the most fascinating thing I've ever seen as Susan's asking me If I've packed condoms. I'm not sure if it's a trick question and I have no idea how to answer. The way I see it, whatever I answer I'm screwed: 'Yes, don't worry I've packed a bumper-sized box' and she thinks I'm a sex-crazed pervert; 'No ma'am, I haven't' and I'm an irresponsible prick.

"Mom, stop. We're not kids. Relax." I want to kiss Blair for jumping in and saving me but I still can't look up.

"Just remember, I'm too young to be made a granny." Her voice is light, but it has an edge to it that tells me she'd deadly serious.

I can't help it, I release a stupidly loud laugh and both women's heads snap to me and I'm done for. I giggle like a twelve-year-old girl and the more I try to stop, the less control I have over it. Blair kicks my foot in a 'shut the hell up' attempt and her mom catches the movement. She shakes her head at me and leaves the room muttering something to herself.

"What the hell was that?" Blair asks incredulously.

"I'm so sorry," I manage to answer though bouts of laughter. "I laugh when I'm nervous…your mom giving us the sex talk made me really anxious."

"She probably thinks you're special now, you know."

I raise an eyebrow. "I am."

"Not that way, idiot…help me put my bags in the car."

"Yes, ma'am." I mock salute and make my way outside while she says goodbye to her mom.

"She said to tell you that if you get me pregnant she'll put a hit out on you," Blair announces as she gets into the car and buckles up.

"I don't doubt that for a second, Princess."

"Good, because she knows people."

I'm well aware of the daggers her mom was shooting at me as I brought Blair's luggage out. The thought that she might put a hit out on me doesn't actually sound that far-fetched.

"Guess I'll just have to double bag it then," I say with a wink.

"Ewww, gross!"

"Whatever, you love it. So…you ready to go?"

"I am," she says around a huge grin as she flicks the radio on and fiddles with the dial.

She settles on a station and leans her seat back, resting her feet on the dash. My eyes trace the length of her legs and notice her summer dress is bunching up at her thighs. I'm hard already and we're not even off of her street. Shit. This is going to be one long ride.

Chapter 33

Blair

WE'RE AT A gas station in the ass end of nowhere be-cause I needed to pee. I'm looking at the rusty little old toilet key attached to a massive metal trash can lid, won-dering to myself if I could maybe hold on until the next services.

"What you waiting for?" Ethan asks, emerging from the store chewing on red vines. I look across to the grub-by-looking toilet blocks and then back to him.

"I don't dare go in."

"What, why?"

"Look at this place!" I whisper shout, "I'm probably gonna get murdered or raped if I go in there. I'm sure I saw something like this in a movie, you know… Girl stops at rundown services, asks to use the bathroom then she's in there all of two minutes and when she comes out, she's murdered by some weird trucker who's been following her for the last hundred miles."

"Wow!"

"What? It could happen."

"That's a pretty impressive imagination you got yourself there, little lady."

I suppress a grin when I notice his whole mouth has been dyed red by the candy.

"I'm standing right here, Princess, nobody will come in."

"But what if there's somebody already lurking about inside, huh? Or a window at the back they could get in through?"

He raises his brows and looks at me like I've been smoking crack.

"Want me to come in with you?"

I look from him, to the ridiculous key in my hand, to the grubby toilet block.

"Yes."

He smiles and lets out an amused chuckle, taking the key from me. I watch from behind his back as he unlocks the door to take a look around inside.

"All clear in here, come on in."

I need to pee so bad that I'm trying to hold my legs together and walk at the same time. I pass him and shuffle into the cubicle, quickly locking the door and dropping my panties. The room's completely silent and I realize that if I pee now, Ethan will definitely be able to hear it.

I'm torn because I don't want him to leave me in here on my own, but at the same time, I'm nowhere near comfortable with him listening to me going to the toilet. There are lines that shouldn't be crossed in a new relationship and I'm pretty sure this is one of them.

"Ethan?"

"Yeah?"

"I can't go, it's too quiet; you'll hear me pee."

The room suddenly fills with his laughter and I want to go back out and junk punch him. "It's not funny, asshole! I'm desperate."

"Well, then, just go."

"What part did you not just understand? Can you make some noise or something? I know, sing. Really loud."

"What? Blair you're being ridiculous."

I'm about to cry. I need to go so bad it hurts. I hear him exhale dramatically and shuffle about.

"I can't believe I'm doing this…. *Happy Birthday to you, Happy Birthday to you...*" I can't help but giggle as the room fills with the sound of him singing.

"Babe, why are you singing *Happy Birthday*?" I shout.

"Why are you not peeing? It's the first song that came into my head; forgive me for not having a set list prepared for bathroom serenades. Now hurry up and go!" He shouts back before starting to sing *Happy Birthday* again.

AS SOON AS the door opens and I step out from the cubicle the singing stops. We eye each other for a moment shrouded in an awkward silence.

"Tell anyone about this and I'll kill you!" I narrow my eyes for effect. I have a pretty good feeling that this won't make it on the things to brag about list.

We stare at each other for a few seconds before my resolve breaks and I can feel the smile I'm trying to hide make an appearance. That's all it takes for Ethan to throw his head back and laugh his ass off. I'm laughing, too, at how stupid this situation is. I walk over to the basin and run my hands under the freezing cold water.

"You know, whenever I've dreamt about guys singing to me, it's never been *Happy Birthday* in a toilet block at some gross truck stop to drown out the sound of me peeing. I feel kind of cheated out of my fantasy," I tell him as he's struggling to regain his composure.

"I'm sorry I didn't quite meet the fantasy. I suppose you could always tell me some more and see if I can live up to those."

"You're a perv, Ethan Jamison. How do you always manage to make things sound so sexual?"

"It's a gift," he says, winking at me and placing his hand to the base of my back before guiding me outside.

"Besides, this one will be fun to tell the grandkids." He takes the ridiculous key and lid out of the door and heads back towards the store to hand it in.

I'm standing frozen to the spot. *Tell the grandkids.* I'm all kinds of giddy that he's contemplated a future for us that involves grandchildren. I look back towards his retreating form and mentally high-five myself that I've found a keeper.

elle

Five hours is a long time to be in a car with someone and not get bored. I appreciate that, really I do. But if Ethan tells me he's bored one more time, I may have to eject him from the car while it's still moving.

"Can we play another game?" he asks, turning the volume down on the radio. We've already exhausted I Spy, Have you Ever and the Yes and No game. The volume display flashes to number fifteen and he pulls his hand away and places it back on the steering wheel.

I look to the display, then to Ethan, then back to the display again. I tell myself to leave it and place my hands under my thighs. I am literally itching to reach out to the volume controller and change it. I bounce my legs up and down a few times then look at display again and finally back to Ethan. He's watching me from the corner of his eye as he's driving. He looks amused. Asshole.

"I can't take it!" I announce. "You can't leave it on an odd number." I lean forward and adjust the dial to read sixteen.

Ethan's wearing a shit-eating grin and mouthing 'weirdo' to himself. If it weren't for the fact that I think we'd probably crash and die since he's driving, I'd punch him.

"I'm not a weirdo, I just don't like things set on odd numbers."

"And that makes you completely normal and not weird at all."

"Absolutely!"

"How did I not notice this about you?" he muses. "Okay…so me doing this won't bother you if you're not a weirdo." He switches the volume to seventeen and sits back looking smug. I'm nothing if not stubborn and I don't want him to know how much the fact that he's just done that, drives me crazy. I lean back and feign indifference to his actions.

"Eat your words smart-ass. Leave it on seventeen for all I care."

We drive for fifteen minutes without speaking to each other, listening to the radio before I cave.

"Ugh, you win Ethan, put it on sixteen before I start having palpitations."

"You lasted way longer than I thought you would, I didn't realize you were one of those O.C.D. types. I bet that was killing you, wasn't it?"

"I hate how well you know me."

"I love how well I know you."

His words make my stomach flutter. I wonder if he'll always make me feel like this. I look over at him and he's still grinning, although he's focusing on the road ahead. His hair's messed up and his shirt's crumpled from the seatbelt. Even so, this is the most beautiful I've ever seen him. He looks carefree, happy and I want to do a little dance that I may have played a part in that smile he's wearing.

"Do you want to play a game or not?" he asks, drumming his fingers on the steering wheel. "What dinosaur would you rather be?"

I scrunch my face in confusion. "What kind of question is that?"

"It's just a random question, but it tells a lot about someone's personality."

"What, like if they actually know the name of a dinosaur, it tells you they're a geek?"

"Just answer the question, Princess."

"Ugh, fine. Okay, a Velociraptor, I guess."

"See, that wasn't so hard, was it? Interesting choice."

"What does it say about me, then? Let me guess…

that I'm small and vicious?"

"I would say that it makes you quick-witted and intelligent," he tells me. I smile internally at my choice in dinosaurs before he's finished. "Also confirms that you're a geek. Nine out of ten people would have said T-Rex; the fact that you know more than one dinosaur proves it."

A groan escapes my lips as I push myself further back into my seat.

"I can't believe I have to spend another five hours in this car with you…god, why was I even looking forward to this?" I press the side of my head to the window and sigh. "You suck at car games," I tell him, although the smile I'm trying to hide is apparent in my voice.

"Are you trying to tell me you'd rather be somewhere else?" he says playfully, although there's an air of uncertainty to it. How he can be unsure that I'm not exactly where I want to be, and with the only person I ever want to share boring car journeys with is beyond me. I need to squash that doubt away.

Chapter 34

Ethan

SHIT, THAT STINGS. I rub my eye and hope to fuck that she didn't just see that. I hear her choke on the laughter she's trying to hold back and I sigh; of course she saw that. I toss the tent pole that just attacked me, snapping back at fucking warp speed and slapping me straight across the eye, and turn to her.

She cocks her head pouting, "Aw, poor baby, did someone not get his camping badge in Cub Scouts?" She's speaking in a baby voice, mocking me and loving every second of it. We've been at the campsite about forty-five minutes and the tent's still not erected. I'm losing at life right now.

"There is no way that pole fits in there!" I point to the sorry excuse of a tent that's flapping about in the wind, taunting me.

"Want me to have a go?"

"No offense, but there's no use, it's the wrong size

pole. If I can't make it fit, there's no sense in letting you mess with it and hurt yourself."

Anyone would think I'd just told her that her ass looks fat in her shorts and her hair's a mess. Her eyes have almost closed completely into slits.

"Move over, cupcake, I want to actually be able to sleep in this thing tonight." She pushes past me and starts dismantling the part of the tent that was already construct-ed. That's just great, now when she can't put it up, I'll have to start from scratch.

"Knock yourself out, Princess."

I sit on the hood of the Camaro and prepare myself to enjoy the show she's about to put on for me when she bends over to fix the tent.

It takes her six and a half minutes; I want to punch myself in the face at how easy she just made that look. I feel completely emasculated. There's a war going on in my head and I'm not sure what emotion is winning out: pride that she schooled me big time, or shame that she schooled me big time. I'm just thankful the band hasn't seen this; they'd burn my man card right here and now in front of me, never mind revoking it.

She saunters toward me looking like that cat that just got the cream; her smile is so wide you'd think she swal-lowed a clothes hanger.

"Yeah, yeah…you're better than me. Blah. Blah. Blah. Please let's not ever speak of this again, okay?"

Her smile stretches even wider. "Are you freaking kidding me? I've already updated Facebook!"

"You're joking, right?"

The gleam in her eye lets me know that she's not.

"Fuck's sake, Blair!" I pull her between my legs and rest my hands on her hips. "The guys are gonna eat this shit up. Thanks for that."

"Quit your whining, grab the sleeping bags and let's go to bed."

All thoughts of the guys dissolve at her words. My mind flashes to the last time we spent the night together and I feel my jeans tighten as she looks up at me from under her lashes.

"Yes, ma'am."

𝓮𝓵𝓮

Of all the fantasies I've had over the past few weeks about this night, none of them involved what I'm witnessing right now. The sleeping bags are positioned on the floor and Blair is sitting Indian-style pulling clothes from her bag to put on.

"Princess, I was kinda hoping you'd be taking your clothes off."

"Relax, I'm just looking for something to sleep in, it's colder than I was expecting."

"I can think of a few ways to warm you up." I lunge forward knocking her onto her back and positioning myself over her.

"You're an idiot," she giggles.

"You're right, I've let you stay clothed for way too long." I wink and then begin unbuttoning her shirt, my fingers trembling with the desire and need that she elicits in me. I lower my face to hers and I push my fingers into her hair. I place a kiss on the tip of her nose and then remove her glasses and place kisses over each eyelid. I can feel her heart beating against my chest and I think it's my new favorite thing.

Her mouth moves to make contact with my own as she runs her hands over my back, pulling me down onto her harder. The awareness of her body pressed against mine has me pulling at her shirt, wanting to feel her skin against me, minus the barrier of our clothes. She shrugs out of it only breaking the kiss to allow me to pull my t-shirt up over my head.

We resume our positions, only this time it's skin on skin and I can feel her trembling beneath me. We are a mess of tangled limbs and desperate kisses, our hands frantically exploring one another. I break away and reach over to my backpack to retrieve a condom. I'm pulling out everything I packed looking for them; I know I packed them I just can't seem to find where.

"There's a pack in my bag," Blair offers.

"You brought condoms?"

"Wasn't sure if you'd bring enough." She smiles and I want to say to hell with the protection and just take her now.

I move over and start looking through her bag. I pull out a few items of clothing along with her camera and a notebook, placing them on the floor besides me. I find her toiletry bag and the pack of condoms nestled neatly in the side. Thank god. I place her clothes and camera back into the bag and pick up the notebook to do the same. A bunch of papers fall out, fluttering slowly to the ground and land where I'm kneeling. I open the book to place the papers back within it and pause when I notice my name. I look from the book to Blair and back down at the book again. My heart rate accelerates as I pull out the list that's nestled between the pages and read down it. My stomach rolls and I shake my head, willing the words I'm seeing to somehow magically change before me. I look to Blair but she's frozen, watching and waiting for my reaction.

"Is this some kind of joke?"

"Ethan, it's not what you think."

I let out a laugh that's anything but humorous and feel a cold chill run down my spine.

"Really Blair? Because it looks like Emily's list to me, and funnily enough I've been singled out on it." I look again at the purple writing in front of me. #10. Lose my V card (Ideally Ethan Jamison!) It's been crossed off the list, just like everything else except Visit Vegas, The Grand Canyon and Fall in love. Shit.

"Did you plan on getting to know me so you could sleep with me for this fucking list?"

She flinches at my words and I'd probably feel bad for it if she hadn't just ripped my heart out.

"What? Of course not! Don't be stupid."

"Stupid's a goddamn understatement, Blair. You slept with me to cross off a stupid point on a list that someone else made."

I stand as best I can in this stupid fucking tent and pull my t-shirt back on. I need to get out of here and get some air; I can't breathe. I unzip the door and walk outside while Blair scrambles behind me to put her shirt back on. I kick at the dirt with my toe and work my jaw back and forth. I can feel my eyes start to prickle with tears and I hold by head back, looking up towards the sky as I try my best to keep them in check. I don't know what's gutted me more, the fact that I was probably just a point to cross off for her, or that she didn't cross off that she's fallen in love.

"Ethan, it's really not what you think. Please let me explain."

"What's left to explain? That list was pretty clear." I can hear the blood rushing in my ears. I don't want to listen to anything that she says at the moment. I trusted her, told her things about my life that I've never said out loud to another person. I fell in love with her, and for what? It's all been a huge lie. I've probably been one massive inconvenience in this whole fucked up experiment, or whatever the hell this is.

"Emily made that list for her, not me. She wanted to do those things before she died. She had a crush on you for years—that's why your name was on the list. She wanted you to be her first."

I take a deep breath and walk over to my car; I sit on the hood and rest my elbows on my knees. I'm so tired of feeling like shit. I want to believe that I'm not just some pawn in her stupid bucket list game but I'm not sure that I do. I don't know how to respond to her last statement so I don't. I'm not even sure I could if I wanted to, my throat feels like it's closing up, burning at the effort I'm making to not bawl like a fucking baby. Since meeting Blair I've never once thought she'd be able to make me feel this bad with almost no effort. I look up to see her watching me. Her face is stained with tears and as bad as I'm feeling right now, as much as I'm mad at her, I'm fucking furious with myself. Seeing her upset guts me more than I can take, I shouldn't be feeling bad for her. She got caught.

"I didn't ever plan to pursue you because of her list, I

swear."

"But you just couldn't help yourself when you had to tutor me, is that it? You saw your chance and took it."

"No of course not, everything that has happened between us is real, Ethan, everything. Not because of Em, or because I wanted to fulfill a promise I made."

"If that's true, then why did you bother to cross it off the list? If you slept with me for you and not her?" I can feel a hot trail make its way down my cheek as a rogue tear escapes. "I've been such a stupid prick! I thought that you felt the same way I did. I'm fucking in love with you and it's all fake to you. It's the only thing you didn't cross off!" I don't give her time to respond as I hop off the hood and round the car, getting in and cranking the engine.

"Wait, Ethan, that's not true!" I hear her call out as I put the car in reverse, she's all-out crying now and I need to get away. I maneuver the car away from her and watch as she starts to run towards me and I snap. I can feel the exact moment my heart shatters. The ache in my chest hurts infinitely more than any of the beatings my dad's ever doled out. I quickly put the car in drive and speed away from the one thing in my life that I thought was good.

Chapter 35

Blair

"HE LEFT ME," I say the words out loud in a state of shock. I'm standing in the middle of the freaking desert at some random campsite alone, crying. He didn't even let me explain. I'm not sure what I'm upset most about, the fact that he found the list and freaked, or the fact that he's abandoned me.

My glasses have steamed up and my shirt's buttoned up wrong. I look a mess. I feel a mess. I rub at my arms to ward of a chill that's settled over me at the prospect of Ethan not returning. Shit, what if he doesn't come back for me?

I'm hating myself for not showing him the list sooner and explaining. I'd brought it with me deluded by some silly notion that it would be like having Em here with me to share this. I even had in the back of my mind that I would explain the list fully to him this weekend—when or if the right moment arose. But then, why should I have? It was Emily's list and letter, addressed to me and no one else.

I walk back to the tent and climb inside, zipping it up and using the little padlock I brought to secure it. I wasn't particularly scared with Ethan here but I'm suddenly all too aware that I'm alone. I want to call my mom and tell her what's happened, but it will just worry her and I'm hoping like hell that he's just going to drive around for a little while, calm down and then come back. I take my cell out and try to call his number but it diverts straight to voicemail. I decide to leave him a text instead.

To: Ethan
Please come back and let me explain.
I promise it's not as bad as you think. B xx

I hit send and then spend the next twenty minutes staring continuously at my phone, but he hasn't replied. I try to call a few more times and each time it's the same thing. I've left two voice messages and now I'm really starting to worry that he has just abandoned me here.

My cell screen lights up and my heart almost leaps out of my chest until I notice it's my mom calling. What the hell am I going to say to her?

I hit the accept button and put her on speaker.

"Hey, Mom."

"Hi, sweetie, I'm just checking that you've arrived safely. You know me, I'd have never slept tonight if I hadn't heard from you."

My stomach bottoms out and I start to feel nauseated. She's gonna flip her top.

"We got here fine, Mom. Listen, I need to tell you

something but you have to promise that you're not gonna freak out, okay?"

"Jesus Christ, Blair, don't ever start a sentence like that! Now you know I'm going to freak."

"Ethan's left." I say the words and they're followed by a long silence, so long that I think the call may have disconnected. "Mom, did you hear me? Mom?"

"What do you mean, 'Ethan's left'? What, like he's left you on your own? So help me god if he's disappeared on you in the middle of nowhere I'll rip that boy's head clean off." Her voice has raised a few octaves and I can tell she's trying to remain calm.

"We had an argument. Well, not really an argument. He found a letter from Emily in my things and got upset and left."

"Okay, so why would he get upset about a letter? What haven't you told me, Blair? And don't leave any-thing out now, I want the truth."

I sigh audibly and resign myself to the fact that I need to explain the whole list and letter to my mom who has no clue about any of it. Suddenly I feel like a little child that's been caught with her hand in the cookie jar. I tell her all about when nurse Carla came to see me and left me the letter. I tell her about the list and all the things on it that Emily wanted me to do for her. I even tell her about the fact that I crossed off 'losing my virginity' but not 'falling in love', and then sit in silence and wait for the onslaught to begin. It doesn't, though; in fact if anything, she sounds upset.

"Baby girl, why didn't you talk to me about this?" I can hear the disappointment in her tone and it only makes me feel worse.

"And say what? You'd have only told me not to do it, and right now I'm wishing I hadn't but it's done. I can't change that he thinks I've slept with him because of Em, and I can't change that I haven't told him I love him when he's already told me. Now it's just going to look like a last-ditch attempt to talk myself out of this mess."

My voice breaks and before I can get myself in check I'm crying again.

"Sweetheart, nothing is ever as bad as is first seems. You love him, huh? I suppose I should have known that. Blair, just tell him what you've told me. What's done is done now and there's no sense in regretting it. You need to sit down and discuss this with him like adults. Any fool can see that boy is head over heels for you."

"Yeah, that's great, Mom, except I don't know where he is."

"Hmm, about that. Look honey, stay where you are and if he hasn't gotten in touch or returned in the next hour or so call me back. I'll organize a cab to take you to the airport, I can book you a flight back home."

"You can't do th—"

"I can do what I want, Blair. I'm your mother and I'm not about to leave you stranded in the middle of nowhere, hours from home."

"Okay, I guess I'll call you back soon, then."

"You do that, and Blair?"

"Yeah?"

"I love you."

"I love you too, Mom," I tell her as I end the call and climb into the sleeping bag. I pull Emily's letter out and re-read the purple writing. "This is all your fault," I whisper as I lean back and wait for a text or call that I don't really believe is coming.

ele

The stillness inside of the tent is shattered as I'm jarred awake by my cell ringing. I lunge forward and scramble around between the sleeping bags, frantically trying to get to my phone before the call ends. It's Ethan's ringtone playing. I find it and hit accept.

"Hello, Ethan? Ethan, are you there?"

"Yeah hi, um, I'm looking for a Blair Thomas. Is that you?" The female voice on the end of the line is definitely not my boyfriend's and my stomach churns at all the possible reasons a woman would have his phone.

"Yeah, this is Blair. Who is this, please?"

"Great hi, my name's Mindy. I'm a bartender. I have your boyfriend here in a pretty sorry state. I've taken his keys from him; he was intent on driving but the guy can barely stand. You think you could come collect him? We close in the next hour."

"Yeah sure, I just…um, okay give me the address and I'll be there as soon as I can." My mind's racing wondering how the hell I'm supposed to be able to go get him when I don't have a vehicle. And how the hell did he manage to get himself drunk in some bar? I've seen his fake ID—it's not great.

Mindy reels off the address and I add it to my phone's contacts before calling information for a cab number. It takes a half hour before the cab arrives and then another twenty minutes before we're pulling up alongside one of the seediest looking bars I've ever seen. I really don't want to have to go in, but I don't have much of a choice. I notice Ethan's car in the lot, so I know I'm definitely at the right place.

I make my way inside the grubby bar; it's dull and humid and my sneakers are sticking to the wooden floor. The air is thick with the smell of stale beer and tobacco, and I feel like I'm in a scene from a movie as everyone seems to stop and stare at me with a 'what the hell are you doing in here' look. I'm almost positive someone cut the music the second I stepped inside. I can see Ethan slumped over the end of the bar with his head resting on his arms. A blonde bartender with way too much make-up and far too few clothes on notices me and makes her way over.

"Just a hunch, but I'm guessing you're Blair?" she asks as she leans over the bar, giving me a perfect view of her over inflated chest that will probably haunt me for weeks to come.

"Yeah, how long's he been like this?" I point over to where Ethan is currently passed out.

"Oh, a couple of hours at least. Poor boy came in with a face like thunder, started hitting the Jack real hard. After a few drinks he loosened up some and told me all about some girl that had broken his heart. He seemed pretty cut up, carried on drinking and then before I knew it, he was three sheets to the wind and couldn't stand up. Here you go, sugar." She fishes under the bar and then passes over Ethan's car keys. All the while she's been talking Ethan hasn't raised his head to acknowledge my presence.

"Thanks for calling me and not letting him drive." I offer a weak smile and walk over to Ethan and gently shake his shoulder.

"Ethan, wake up baby. We need to go." He raises his head and squints to bring me into focus.

"What do you want? Are you here to finish me off? Make sure you broke my heart right?" There's a coldness to his eyes that makes my heart hurt. He really believes that I don't love him.

"I'm here to drive you back to the camp. Come on and help me out would you? Stand up." He shuffles around until he finally slips off the stool and comes to a very unsteady stand. His eyes are glazed over and he smells like a whiskey barrel. I position his arm over my shoulder and begin slowly walking him out of the bar as I hear Mindy call time.

"You know you're kind of a bitch," he tells me as we're almost to his car. "You played me."

"Hey now, that's no way to talk to a lady!" a deep voice booms from behind us, and I look back to see a huge burly guy in a plaid shirt and cowboy boots making his way towards us.

"You're a pretty little thing, ain't ya? Why don't you leave your friend here and come have a drink with me?"

"No, I'm good, thanks," I begin to respond as Ethan interjects.

"Hey asshole, don't be speaking to my girlfriend like that!" he practically sneers.

"Your girlfriend, huh? Say, miss, why don't you ditch this loser and I'll show you what a real man's like?"

I don't get chance to process a response before Ethan's arm is flying past my face and connecting with the asshole's behind us. The whole thing pans out before me in painfully slow motion as I'm thrown to the side and

Ethan's head snaps back from the guy's return punch.

The bar is closing and the few guys that were inside are making their way out. Before I know what's happening someone shouts, "What's going on?" And I'm suddenly surrounded by a bunch of guys trying to diffuse the fight. One of the men trying to break things up gets hit in the face and then suddenly all hell breaks loose and everyone seems to be joining in. It's one huge free-for-all as people are trading punches while I'm frantically screaming Ethan's name to get his attention so we can get away.

I don't see the elbow coming towards me until it's too late and I feel searing hot pain shoot through my cheek-bone as I stumble back and land on my ass. Ethan is in-stantly beside me grabbing at me to check if I'm okay. I scream for him to move just as some guy hits him across the back of the head with a bottle sending him falling to the ground out cold beside me. I'm not sure how long it is that I'm sitting nursing his head in my lap before he grog-gily opens his eyes and murmurs unintelligibly to me.

I stare down at the blood slowly dripping from Ethan's nose and I'm instantly reminded of the last time I saw blood. If I close my eyes I can hear Emily's voice in my head right now.

"How do I look?" she asked twirling around in front of her bedroom mirror. She was wearing a midnight blue, floor-length strapless gown and looked breathtaking. The dark material was a stark contrast to her pale skin.

"You look amazing," I answered with a smile. "If you were ever going to make a play for Ethan Jamison, you should do it in that dress."

"You know what? I think tonight may be the night.

This is most likely going to be the last winter formal I attend. I'm making the most of it."

I attempted a weak smile as her words registered. Every time I let myself remember that her illness was terminal and that she was living on borrowed time, I felt a part of me shatter. I was done crying in front of her, though. I didn't know how long she had left, and I wouldn't spend a second not being upbeat and trying to keep her smiling.

"Let's go down and let your mom and dad take a billion photos and get out of here."

"Wait, I need to fix my hair!" she said laughing, and then my smile was genuine. Her hair was in a super short pixie cut, she licked the palm of her hand, smoothed it across her head and wiggled her eyebrows. "Done!"

I shook my head in amusement as we made our way downstairs and were bombarded by camera flashes.

"You two look beautiful," Bill told us and after the obligatory curfew and stay safe, don't drink, drive careful talk we were finally out of the door and on our way to our winter formal.

ele

We arrived at the school gym that had been decorated in a ton of silver and white tinsel. Fake snow had been laid out and snowflake decorations adorned every surface in sight. We headed straight to the dance floor and Em was in her element as I swayed awkwardly from side to side. I'd never been great in social situations and I definitely preferred not to dance, but if Em was having fun I'd suck it *up. We danced for what seemed like hours but I'm sure it was only minutes. Em stumbled and reached out for my arm,*

"Shit, are you ok?" I asked her, taking note of her expression.

"Yeah, I'm fine, I just need to sit down I think, I'm a little dizzy."

I took her arm and guided her to one of the bench seats that lined the perimeter of the room and we sat down watching the crowd, as she concentrated on taking deep calming breaths.

"You feel better now?"

"Yeah, a little bit. I guess I just overdid it." Her voice tapered off as her eyes locked on to Ethan Jamison, walking towards the halls.

"You know what, Blair? I'm gonna make a move; he can only say no, right?"

My smile was huge as I nodded my agreement. "Definitely!"

She smoothed her dress down ready to go and make her play on the guy that she'd crushed on forever and I felt so proud. My happiness was short lived though, as her body went limp and she tumbled to the floor in front of me with blood trickling from her nose. The teachers called an ambulance and we were transported through to the hospital, but it was all a blur. Before I knew what had happened, we were sitting in the Teenage Cancer Unit common room with Em hooked up to an IV of platelets, dressed in evening gowns and heels.

"This is not how this night was supposed to go," she commented dejectedly. "I'm supposed to be being felt up behind the gym, not stuck in here with this." She grabbed

a hold of the IV stand and rattled it.

"I'd be happy to feel you up?" a deep voice echoed from behind us and we both spun around wide-eyed to see who had offered their groping services.

My eyes landed on a tall tanned guy with buzzed brown hair and a lip ring through his plump bottom lip. He was wearing a snug black t-shirt and tight black jeans, like a super hot Emo guy. I nudged Em's shoulder and whispered under my breath, "I'd let him!"

She burst out laughing and the guy stood unmoving and staring at Em like she was candy and he was a baby. It took a minute to realize that he too was holding an IV stand that he seemed to be hooked up to.

"This is gonna sound weird but I saw you come in, and I figured that life's too short right? I need to tell you that you're the hottest girl I think I've ever seen," Emo hottie stated.

My jaw literally hit the floor, as Em played all coy and shy.

"Wow, he's smooth," I laughed as he shot me a brilliant white smile. I took it as my cue to leave and grab a coffee while Em and Emo hottie made friends.

ele

"Okay Blair, I didn't just dream that up right? Lucas was real wasn't he?" Emily asked as I walked back into the common room thirty minutes later. Em's parents were hot on my heels.

"If by Lucas you mean Emo hottie, nope! He was very real." I smiled.

"Excellent, well this shitty night just got a whole lot better. That means I didn't just imagine that kiss or his number in my cell."

"You did not just kiss him!" I whisper shouted as Pam and Bill walked up beside us to greet her. She smiled huge and wiggled her eyebrows."

"Oh my god, you did!"

"Did what, honey?" Pam asked.

"Nothing," Em smirked.

"I'm so sorry, honey, this must have been a horrible night for you."

"Actually, no," she replied. "It's been pretty awesome."

I take in the sight of Ethan in front of me now, and I know that this night is destined for many things, but awesome isn't one of them.

Police cars begin to pull up and cops are hauling people aside. We're loaded into the back of a cruiser and being read our rights as I try to process that this is all really happening. I can't help thinking that it's entirely my fault. If I had just shown the list to him and explained it in the first place, we wouldn't be in this mess now.

Chapter 36

Ethan

TO SAY THAT I feel rough would be the understatement of the fucking century. My back is aching and my head feels like it's about to explode. I open my eyes and am greeted with the sight of a concrete ceiling, not the fabric of a tent I was expecting. I lay still for a second before my memory catches up with me. I dart forward looking around for Blair, but I'm in a cell on my own and she's nowhere to be seen.

"Blair!" I shout as I stand and make my way shakily to the door and look through the tiny opening.

"Ethan, I'm here." Her voice echoes and I look out the through the opening again and notice she's doing the same in the cell opposite me. Thank god. My heart rate begins to slow as I realize she's not missing.

"Are you okay?" I shout and I can just make out the scowl on her face as she replies.

"What do you think?" She sounds as if she wants to

kill me. In all honesty I don't blame her. I kind of want to die right now myself.

"How's your head?" she asks in the most pissed tone I've ever heard her use, and I immediately feel bad until I remember the list and then the guilt subsides and gives way to anger.

"It's fine," I bite out, and her expression hardens even more if that's possible. The tension ramps up a million points.

"Really? That's all you've got to say to me?" She's watching me and I see her eyebrows rise as she waits for me to respond. When I don't she carries on. "First, you run off and leave me by myself in the middle of a campsite in the desert. You don't answer my calls or texts to let me explain that what you think you know is all bullshit. Then you go get trashed at a bar and get us into a brawl that's resulted in a nice little impromptu stay at the jailhouse! Even after all this…you're looking at me like it's you that has the right to be pissed!" She huffs, closing her eyes and shaking her head in obvious disgust before moving away from the door so I can't see her anymore.

"Look, I'm sorry for the fact that you're sitting in here now, but you know what? I kind of do feel justified at being pissed with you." This gets her attention and her face re-appears at the door, eyes narrowed.

"I'm in love with a girl who's dating me for her dead best friend's bucket list Blair, how do you think that makes me feel? Seeing that list and all the things you did and didn't cross off?" Her gaze softens slightly as I hear her exhale loudly.

"Ethan, what you read has no bearing on what we have. I never intended to sleep with you just so that I could cross it off the list. I gave you my virginity because I'm in love with you, because you're smart and funny and sweet and you make me feel cherished. Not because it was written on Emily's list. I crossed it off and immediately wanted to uncross it because I slept with you for me, no one else. I didn't cross off that I'd fallen in love because it's not my list. It's Em's; it felt wrong putting a strike through the 'losing my virginity' point and so I decided not to cross off the other. That is the only reason it has been left blank, I swear." Her eyes are teary as she presses her face closer to the door.

"I am beyond in love with you, I wanted to tell you so many times but I didn't know how to go about it, and then you said it first and I didn't want you to think that I was only saying it back because you'd said it first."

"Blair I do—"

"No—let me finish, okay? I am in love with you. I have been since you took care of me after TJ's party. You're this amazingly strong guy who has to deal with some pretty shitty stuff and you just get on with it. God, I don't know what else to say to make you realize what you mean to me and—"

"Stop!" I interrupt. "I'm sorry, Princess," I say quietly. "For leaving you at the campsite, getting us into this mess. I never wanted this to happen. I just saw the list and I don't think I've ever felt pain like that. I should have let you explain but I couldn't stand how much it hurt, that this," I motion with my hand between us through the opening, "wasn't real. I'm so damn sorry, Princess."

I'd give anything to be able to wrap my arms around her right now, rest my chin on her head and just breathe her in. The silence is broken and the moment lost to the sound of a cop walking between the cell doors, telling us that we're being bailed. I look to Blair with obvious confusion because she answers my question without me having to speak it.

"We've been here all night, you were asleep for almost eleven hours. I could hear you snoring from in here. I must have lost my cell when the fight broke out so I couldn't call my mom. I don't have it memorized as stupid as that sounds." She moves into the hall as the cop opens her door and she looks at me with a worried expression. "I didn't know what else to do so I got your mom's number from your phone and called her."

Fuck. "That's fine princess," I say as calmly as I can manage. I'm just mentally praying that mom hasn't told my dad.

elle

We are both led out into a separate room where some overweight tired-looking older cop fills paperwork out for us while handing me back my keys, cell and wallet.

"Lucky for you two, you have connections," he says looking us both up and down. "All charges brought against you have been dropped."

I feel a chill run down my spine at the word connections that can only mean one thing. My dad knows. I look at Blair and she must be having the same thoughts judging by the look on her face. I give her a smile, attempting to reassure her that everything is okay, but I don't believe that for a second. We both have to sign some paperwork before being ushered out into the reception area where sure enough, my dad is leaning against a desk waiting. He looks completely furious, his arms are crossed over his chest and his gaze is narrowed. He glances from me to Blair and then back to me again with nothing but disappointment and anger in his eyes. There's no 'hello', no 'how are you?' No pleasantries at all. He turns and walks out, expecting us to follow silently, and that's exactly what we do.

Blair has my hand in a death grip as we walk towards what I'm assuming is a rental. Dad opens the back door and stands aside to let us both in. His jaw is working back and forth and I'm sure that if I were on my own right now he wouldn't be so quiet. Blair climbs in and he closes the door, stopping me from following.

"You've got some explaining to do once your girl-friend's gone," he tells me in an eerily calm voice.

"Yes, sir," I answer and make my way around to the other side of the vehicle and get in.

The car smells ridiculously strongly of lemon air freshener, and I don't know if it's because I'm already not feeling too good, but I find the smell nauseating and over-powering. I'm hung-over, I can still taste whisky and my head aches like it's being squeezed in a vice. The morning sunlight is streaming through the windshield and stinging my eyes; no matter how I try to arrange the visor it offers no relief. We drive in silence for about ten minutes before my dad's resolve breaks.

"What the hell happened? I'm dying to know why I had to get on a plane and come bail your sorry ass out of jail. You'd better have a damn good explanation." His voice cuts through the already frigid atmosphere in the car and I see Blair tense from the corner of my eye.

"It was my fault, Mr. Jamison. A guy came onto me at a bar and Ethan was just trying to protect me." My head snaps to Blair's and she's pleading me with her eyes to go along with her story. She's trying to protect me and as much as I love her for doing it. I hate that she feels like she needs to.

"Do I look stupid to you, girl? I was talking to Ethan!" he barks out and Blair flinches back in her seat.

"Don't talk to her like that." I can handle him talking to me like I'm a piece of shit but not her. Never her.

"Who the hell do you think you're talking to? I've just come to bail you and your little whore out and this is how you talk to me?"

I see red and ball my fists at my side. "If you ever call her a whore again I swear to god I'll make you regret it." My words filter into the calm and quiet of the car but they hit their mark as intended. The road we're on is empty, so he pulls to a stop and turns in his seat with his eyes blazing like fire. I know what's coming next; at least I would if we weren't all strapped into a car. This would be the point where he loses his shit and beats the crap out of me until he feels better. Thing is, he can't really do that from where he's sitting and he's not the kind of guy that likes an audience. Blair's eyes are wide as she takes in the stalemate that we've come to.

"What the hell did you just say to me?" he roars and I hear Blair's intake of breath. He's scaring the shit out of her and something in me snaps. I've never had a reason to fight back before until now. Blair has changed that. For the first time in my life I feel like I'm worth something. She

256

makes me want to stand up to him, be a man, defend and take care of her. I would rather die than let him upset her.

"You fucking heard me! Don't disrespect her and talk down to her. Your problem is with me, no one else, and you know what? My whole life I've wondered why you seem to hate me so much, put me down, make me feel worthless. Well, now I know. Mom told me about my real mom. What kind of a man does that make you, huh? I'm the only thing you've got left of a woman you supposedly loved, and what do you do? You beat me. Your own flesh and blood; part of you and her. Most people would cherish the only reminder of a person they once loved, but oh no, not you, Dad. No, you preferred to kick and punch and beat the hell out of me for reminding you of her. I can't help how I look, or mannerisms that I may share with her. I've never intentionally tried to bait you or upset you. I've spent my whole fucking life trying to live up to what you expected and it was never going to be good enough, was it? Because what it all boils down to is that you hate me. You hate me for living and reminding you of what you've lost. I'm never going to be able to change that, am I?"

I'm shaking with the surge of adrenaline coursing through my veins. I can hear the blood rushing in my ears and my whole body feels like it's wound tight as a coil, ready to snap at any second.

"Get out the car, now!"

I look to Blair who's shaking her head.

"Guys, you need to calm down," she pleads as we both unbuckle and make a move to exit the car. That's when I see the look of pure horror flash across her face. I hear her scream just as I turn to see the truck heading straight for us and showing no sign of stopping. I throw myself across her to unbuckle her belt but she's frozen to the seat. The sound of squealing tires and blasting horn fills the car seconds before darkness takes over.

I CAN HEAR high-pitched ringing and the sound of an engine running. Someone's shouting but I can't make out who it is. I move my head and try to blink my eyes back into focus. It's hard work. My eyelids feel like they're made of lead; I'm struggling to force them open. I try to lift myself from my position across the foot well at Blair's feet, but I'm engulfed in white-hot pain from every part of my body. Panic sets in as I realize what's happened. "Blair? Princess, can you hear me?" It hurts to speak and I feel like the same kind of winded pain I felt when the ass-hole had broken my ribs two years ago.

I'm met with silence as I try again to lift myself up and see if Blair's okay. I cry out in pain as I manage to prop myself up onto the seat. Blair is still sitting in the same position except her eyes aren't open. An ice-cold dread slides over me and I'm no longer thinking about the pain I'm in.

"Blair, baby…open your eyes. Wake up for me, Prin-cess. Open your eyes." My tears spill out as I lift my arm and start to nudge her. "Blair!" I'm screaming her name this time and still there's no movement. My head's swim-ming and my eyes are begging to close. "Help! Somebody help me!"

I look around and can't see any sign of my dad. The front of the car is completely crumpled, the windshield is smashed and the seat's empty where he was sitting only moments ago.

"Help!" I shout out again but it hurts too badly and I start coughing. I can't breathe properly and I can't wake Blair. I've never been so scared in my life and my eyes are getting heavier by the second. I'm willing them to stay open; they need to be open. I need to wake her.

"Princess, don't leave me. Open your eyes and promise me you won't leave me…please?" I'm shaking her hard now and crying in utter terror. I can hear the sound of sirens but I'm not sure if they're real or if I'm imagining it. The ringing inside my ears is getting louder and I'm fighting a losing battle to stay awake. My tears feel like fire as they spill over my face and I squeeze my eyes shut tight to try stopping them. The sight of Blair laughing as we were pillow fighting enters my mind, the look on her face as I tell her I love her, the sight of her beautiful green eyes gazing into mine as we make love. I can't make myself open my eyes now. I'm cold and I feel strangely weightless. I want to go to sleep but somewhere in the back of my mind I know I shouldn't, but my body isn't responding to the pleas my mind is making.

"Ethan?"

I hear her soft beautiful voice breathe my name as I try and say 'I love you'. I want to take one last look at her but I can't move anymore. I'm being pulled under and I'm powerless to stop it. Her face is the last thing my mind sees as I succumb to darkness.

Thank YOU

WHERE TO START? Okay it most definitely needs to be with an apology. I know with perfect unwavering certainty that I WILL forget to mention people. I have a fantastic ability to retain useless information, but when it comes to the important things like this…I'm a nightmare. So, to all of you people that most definitely deserve a mention and I haven't named you, it wasn't intentional. I'm sorry, thank you for all of your support and encouragement. I'm so very grateful.

I need to thank my amazing family. You have had to patiently endure months of microwave meals, creased clothes and have every single question you've asked, answered with: "let me just finish this paragraph!"

Thank you from the bottom of my heart for allowing me the time and space I needed to write this book. I love you. You are my world.

The next shout out has to be to my partner in crime Author Kathryn Andrews. Your support has been above and beyond anything I could have ever dreamt or hoped for. I look forward to our daily chats and completely random conversations. You've steered me back on course so many times with your notes and little nuggets of encouragement. You are like my own personal life coach! Thank you. I can't wait to toast our books with a ridiculously large glass of pink champagne.

To all the wonderful Bloggers that have reviewed and promoted my work, there are too many of you to name and I'm terrified that if I try, I will miss someone out. So please know that every single one of you is awesome. Your help has been invaluable. You all took a chance on a new indie and I'm indebted to you forever.

My BETA girls! *Jaime, Silvia, Malinda, Dana, Bobbi* and *Sue,* I sent you out my manuscript and was so nervous for your comments, it felt like I had mailed you all nude pictures of myself! Sharing my book with you left me feeling completely exposed, but then I started to receive your comments and WOW. I had hoped that you would like the book; I never expected you to all come back and tell me that you loved it. Your suggestions and encouragement gave me the confidence to push forward and publish. I can never thank you all enough.

My proofreaders, *Olivia (Rosie), and Mary Lou* - what can I say? Except autocorrect hates me! You guys have been amazing.

The wonderfully talented *Melissa Gill* of MGBOOK-COVERS & DESIGNS. You took my ideas and produced exactly what I had been envisaging in my mind. The cover is beautiful and I can't wait to see what you come up with for book #2.

Marie Piquette editor extraordinaire, I feel like I should both apologize to you for the horrendous amount of run-ons, and thank you for your time and patience. You are a STAR!

Julie (JT Formatting) my brilliant formatter, thank you for working your magic. You transformed my manuscript into a beautiful book.

Finally a huge thank you to you the reader, it is still blowing my mind that you're reading my words. I hope you continue to follow the path I've mapped out for Blair and Ethan as their story concludes in book #2 of The Promises Series.

For information about Elle Brooks and her books, visit:

Her Blog:

http://ellebrooksauthor.wix.com/blog

Twitter:

https://twitter.com/@ellebrooksautho

e-mail:

ellebrooksauthor@gmail.com

Facebook:

https://www.facebook.com/elle.brooks.author